HENRY BROCKEN

His Travels & Adventures in the Rich, Strange, Scarce-Imaginable Regions of Romance

by WALTER de la MARE

NEW YORK · MCMXXIV
ALFRED · A · KNOPF

Set up, electrotyped, and printed by the Vail-Ballou Press, Inc., Binghamton, N. Y.
Paper furnished by W. F. Etherington & Co., New York.
Bound by the Plimpton Press, Norwood. Mass.

MANUFACTURED IN THE UNITED STATES OF AMERICA

With a heart of furious fancies,
  Whereof I am commander:
    With a burning spear,
    And a horse of air,
  To the wilderness I wander;

With a Knight of ghosts and shadows,
  I summoned am to Tourney:
    Ten leagues beyond
    The wide world's end;
  Methinks it is no journey.
                    ANON. (*Tom o' Bedlam*).

Contents

                                             PAGE

I. WHITHER   15

Come hither, come hither, come hither!
SHAKESPEARE.

II. LUCY GRAY   20

Oft I had heard of Lucy Gray;
And, when I crossed the wild,
I chanced to see at break of day
The solitary child.

III. JANE EYRE   27

I used to rush into strange dreams at night: dreams
... where amidst unusual scenes ... I still again
and again met Mr. Rochester; ... and then the sense
of being in his arms, hearing his voice, meeting his
eye, touching his hand and cheek, loving him, being
loved by him—the hope of passing a lifetime at his side,
would be renewed, with all its first force and fire.
CHARLOTTE BRONTË (*Jane Eyre,* Ch. **xxxii.**).

IV. JULIA, ELECTRA, DIANEME   45

Gather ye rosebuds while ye may,
Old Time is still a-flying:
And this same flower that smiles to-day
To-morrow will be dying.

The glorious Lamp of Heaven, the Sun,
The higher he's a-getting,
The sooner will his race be run,
And nearer he's to setting.

That age is best which is the first,
When youth and blood are warmer;
But being spent, the worse, and worst
Times still succeed the former.

7

Contents

Then be not coy, but use your time;
And while ye may, go marry:
For having lost but once your prime,
You may forever tarry.

ANTHEA—

Now is the time when all the lights wax dim,
And thou, Anthea, must withdraw from him
Who was thy servant. Dearest, bury me
Under the holy-oak or gospel tree; . . .
Or, for mine honour, lay me in that tomb
In which thy sacred relics shall have room:
For my embalming, sweetest, there will be
No spices wanting when I'm laid by thee.
HERRICK (*Hesperides*).

V. NICK BOTTOM   59

BOT. A calendar, a calendar! look in the almanac;
find out moonshine, find out moonshine.
A Midsummer Night's Dream, Act III., Sc. i.

VI. SLEEPING BEAUTY   67

VII. & VIII. LEMUEL GULLIVER   89

I must freely confess that since my last return some
corruptions of my Yahoo nature have revived in me,
by conversing with a few of your species, and particu-
larly those of my own family, by an unavoidable
necessity; else I should never have attempted so absurd
a project as that of reforming the Yahoo race in this
kingdom: but I have done with all such visionary
schemes for ever.—*Gulliver's Letter to his Cousin.*

The first money I laid out was to buy two young
stone horses, which I kept in a good stable, and next
to them the groom is my greatest favourite: for I feel
my spirits revived by the smell he contracts in the
stable.—SWIFT (*A Voyage to the Houyhnhnms,* Ch. xi.).

IX. & X. MISTRUST, OBSTINATE, LIAR, ETC.   118

And as he read he wept and trembled; and not
being able longer to contain, he brake out with a
lamentable cry, saying, "What shall I do?" . . .
The neighbours also came out to see him run; and

Contents

as he ran, some mocked, others threatened, and some
cried after him to return.

ATHEIST—

Now, after awhile, they perceived afar off, one
coming softly and alone, all along the highway, to
meet them.—BUNYAN (*The Pilgrim's Progress*).

XI. LA BELLE DAME SANS MERCI   148

"O what can ail thee, knight-at-arms,
   Alone and palely loitering?
The sedge has withered from the lake,
   And no birds sing.

"O what can ail thee, knight-at-arms,
   So haggard and so woe-begone?
The squirrel's granary is full,
   And the harvest's done."

                        KEATS.

XII. SLEEP AND DEATH   158

Death will come when thou art dead,
   Soon, too soon—
Sleep will come when thou art fled;
   Of neither would I ask the boon
I ask of thee, beloved Night—
Swift be thine approaching flight,
   Come soon, soon!

                  SHELLEY.

XIII. & XIV. A DOCTOR OF PHYSIC   169

Well, well, well,—
. . . God, God forgive us all!
           Macbeth, Act V., Sc. i.

XV. ANNABEL LEE   197

I was a child, and she was a child
   In this kingdom by the sea;
And we loved with a love that was more than love—
   I and my Annabel Lee—
With a love that the winged seraphs of heaven
   Coveted her and me.

            EDGAR ALLAN POE.

9

Contents

PAGE

XVI. CRISEYDE   207

> . . . Love hadde his dwellinge
> With-inne the subtile stremes of hir yën.
> > Book I., 304-5.

> Y-wis, my dere herte, I am nought wrooth,
> Have here my trouthe and many another ooth;
> Now speek to me, for it am I, Criseyde!
> > Book III., 1110-2.

> And fare now wel, myn owene swete herte!
> > Book V., 1421.
> > CHAUCER (*Troilus and Criseyde*).

The Traveller

to

The Reader

THE traveller who presents himself in this little book feels how tedious a person he may prove to be. Most travellers that he ever heard of were the happy possessors of audacity and rigour, a zeal for facts, a zeal for Science, a vivid faith in powder and gold. Who, then, will bear for a moment with an ignorant, pacific adventurer, without even a gun?

He may, however, seem even more than bold in one thing, and that is in describing regions where the wise and the imaginative and the immortal have been before him. For that he never can be contrite enough. And yet, in spite of the renown of these regions, he can present neither map nor chart of them, latitude nor longitude: can affirm

To The Reader

only that their frontier stretches just this side of Dream; that they border Impossibility; lie parallel with Peace.

And since it is his, and only his, journey and experiences, his wonder and delight in these lands that he tells of—a mere microcosm, as it were—he entreats forgiveness of all who love them and their people as much as he loves them—scarce "on this side idolatry."

H. B.

Henry Brocken

Chapter One

Oh, what land is the Land of Dream?

WILLIAM BLAKE.

I LIVED, then, in the great world once, in an old, roomy house beside a little wood of larches, with an aunt of the name of Sophia. My father and mother died a few days before my fourth birthday, so that I can conjure up only fleeting glimpses of their faces by which to remember what love was then lost to me. Both were youthful at death, but my Aunt Sophia was ever elderly. She was keen and just, seldom less than kind; but a child was to her something of a little animal, and it was nothing more. In consequence, well fed, warmly clad, and in freedom, I grew up almost in solitude between my angels, hearkening—with how simple a curiosity—to that everlasting warfare of persuasion and compulsion, terror and delight.

15

Which of them it was that guided me, before even I could read, to the little room dark with holly trees that had been of old my uncle's library, I know not. Perhaps at the instant it chanced there had fallen a breathless truce between them, and I being solitary, my own instinct took me. But having once found that pictured haven, I had found somewhat of content.

I think half my youthful days passed in that low, book-walled chamber. The candles I burned through those long years of evening would deck Alps' hugest fir; the dust I disturbed would very easily fill again the measure that some day shall contain my own; and the small studious thumbmarks that paced, as if my footprints, leaf by leaf of that long journey, might be the history of life's experience in little—from clearer, to clear, to faint—how very faint at last!

I do not remember ever to have been discovered in this retreat. I was (by nature) prompt at meals, and wary to be in bed at my hour, however transitory its occupation might be. Indeed, I very well recollect dawn painting the page my eyes dwelt on, surprising me with its mystery and stealth in a house as silent as the grave.

Thus entertained then by insubstantial society I grew up, and began to be old, before I had yet learned age is disastrous. And it was there, in that cold, bright chamber, one snowy twilight, first suddenly awoke in me an imperative desire for distant lands.

Even while little else than a child I had begun to cast my mind to travel. I doubt if ever Columbus suffered such vexation from an itch to be gone.

But whither?

Now, it seemed clear to me after long brooding and musing that however beautiful were these regions of which I never wearied to read, and however wild and faithful and strange and lovely the people of the books, somewhere the former must remain yet, somewhere, in immortality serene, dwell they whom so many had spent life in dreaming of, and writing about.

17

In fact, take it for all in all, what could these authors have been at, if they laboured from dawn to midnight, from laborious midnight to dawn, merely to tell of what never was, and never by any chance could be? It was heaven-clear to me, solitary and a dreamer; let me but gain the key, I would soon unlock that Eden garden-door. Somewhere yet, I was sure, Imogen's mountains lift their chill summits into heaven; over haunted sea-sands Ariel flits; at his webbed casement next the stars Faust covets youth, till the last trump shall ring him out of dream.

It was on a blue March morning, with all the trees of my aunt's woods in a pale-green tumult of wind, that, quite unwittingly, I set out on a journey that has not yet come to an end.

There was a hint in the air at my waking, I fancied, not quite of mere earth, the perfume of the banners of Flora, of the mould where in melting snow the crocus blows. I looked from my window, and the western clouds drew gravely and loftily in the illimitable air towards the whistling house. Strange trumpets pealed in the wind. Even my poor, aged Aunt Sophia had changed with the universal change; her great, solitary face reminded me of some long-forgotten April.

And a little before eleven I saddled my uncle's old mare Rosinante (poor female jade to bear a name so glorious!), and rode out (as for how many fruitless seasons I had ridden out!), down the stony, nettle-narrowed path that led for a secret mile or more, beneath lindens, towards the hills.

Chapter Two

Still thou art blest compared wi' me!
ROBERT BURNS.

IT is to be wondered at that in so bleak a wind I could possibly fall into reverie. But the habit was rooted deep in me; Rosinante was prosaic and trustworthy; the country for miles around familiar to me as the palm of my hand. Yet so deeply was I involved, and so steadily had we journeyed on, that when at last I lifted my eyes with a great sigh that was almost a sob, I found myself in a place utterly unknown to me.

But more inexplicable yet, not only was the place strange, but, by some incredible wizardry, Rosinante seemed to have carried me out of a March morning, blue and tumultuous and bleak, into the grey sweet mist of a midsummer dawn.

I found that we were ambling languidly

on across a green and level moor. Far away, whether clouds or hills I could not yet tell, rose cold towers and pinnacles into the last darkness of night. Above us in the twilight invisible larks climbed among the daybeams, singing as they flew. A thick dew lay in beads on stick and stalk. We were alone with the fresh wind of morning and the clear pillars of the East.

On I went, heedless, curious, marvelling; my only desire to press forward to the goal whereto destiny was directing me. I suppose after this we had journeyed about an hour, and the risen sun was on the extreme verge of the gilded horizon, when I espied betwixt me and the deep woods that lay in the distance a little child walking.

She, at any rate, was not a stranger to this moorland. Indeed, something in her carriage, in the grey cloak she wore, in her light, insistent step, in the old lantern she carried, in the shrill little song she or the wind seemed singing, for a moment half impelled me to turn aside. Even Rosinante pricked forward her ears, and stooped her gentle face to view more closely this light traveller. And she pawed the ground with her great shoe, and gnawed her bit when I drew rein and leaned forward in the saddle to speak to the child.

"Is there any path here, little girl, that I may follow?" I said.

"No path at all," she answered.

"But how then do strangers find their way across the moor?" I said.

She debated with herself a moment. "Some by the stars, and some by the moon," she answered.

"By the moon!" I cried. "But at day, what then?"

"Oh, then, sir," she said, "they can see."

I could not help laughing at her demure answers. "Why!" I exclaimed, "what a worldly little woman! And what is your name?"

"They call me Lucy Gray," she said, looking up into my face. I think my heart almost ceased to beat.

"Lucy Gray!" I repeated.

"Yes," she said most seriously, as if to herself, "in all this snow."

" 'Snow,' " I said—"this is dewdrops shining, not snow."

She looked at me without flinching. "How else can mother see how I am lost?" she said.

"Why!" said I, "how else?" not knowing how to reach her bright belief. "And what are those thick woods called over there?"

She shook her head. "There is no name," she said.

"But you have a name—Lucy Gray; and you started out—do you remember?—one winter's day at dusk, and wandered on and on, on and on, the snow falling in the dark, till—— Do you remember?"

She stood quite still, her small, serious face full to the east, striving with far-off dreams. And a merry little smile passed over her lips. "That will be a long time since," she said, "and I must be off home." And as if it had been but an apparition of my eyes that had beset and deluded me, she was gone; and I

found myself sitting astride in the full bright-
ness of the sun's first beams, alone.

What omen was this, then, that I should
meet first a phantom on my journey? One
thing only was clear: Rosinante could trust
to her five wits better than I to mine. So leav-
ing her to take what way she pleased, I rode
on, till at length we approached the woods I
had descried. Presently we were jogging
gently down into a deep and misty valley
flanked by bracken and pines, from which is-
sued into the crisp air of morning a most
delicious aromatic smell, that seemed at least
to prove this valley not far remote from
Araby.

I do not think I was disturbed, though I
confess to having been a little amazed to see
how profound this valley was into which we
were descending, yet how swiftly climbed the
sun, as if to pace with us so that we should not
be in shadow, howsoever fast we journeyed. I
was astonished to see flowers of other seasons
than summer by the wayside, and to hear in
June, for no other month could bear such

green abundance, the thrush sing with a February voice. Here too, almost at my right hand, perched a score or more of robins, bright-eyed, warbling elvishly in chorus as if the may-boughs whereon they sat were white with hoarfrost and not buds. Birds also unknown to me in voice and feather I saw, and little creatures in fur, timid yet not wild; fruits, even, dangled from the trees, as if, like the bramble, blossom and seed could live here together and prosper.

Yet why should I be distracted by these things? thought I. I remembered Maundeville and Hithlodaye, Sindbad and Gulliver, and many another citizen of Thule, and was reassured. A man must either believe what he sees, or see what he believes; I know no other course. Why, too, should I mistrust the bounty of the present merely for the scarcity of the past? Not I!

I rode on, and it seemed had advanced but a few miles before the sun stood overhead, and it was noon. We were growing weary, I think, of sheer delight: Rosinante, with her mild face beneath its dark forelock gazing this side, that side, at the uncustomary landscape; and I ever peering forward beneath my hat in eagerness to descry some living creature a little bigger than these conies and squirrels, to prove me yet in lands inhabited. But the sun was wheeling headlong, and the stillness of late afternoon on the woods, when, dusty and parched and heavy, we came to a break in the thick foliage, and presently to a green gate embowered in box.

Chapter Three

Thou are so true, that thoughts of thee suffice
To make dreams truth, and fables histories.
                                        JOHN DONNE.

I DISMOUNTED and, with the nose of my beast in my bosom, stood awhile gazing, in the half-dream weariness brings, across the valley at the dense forests that covered the hills. And while thus standing, doubtful whether to knock at the little gate or to ride on, it began to open, and a great parti-coloured dog looked out on us. There was certainly something unusual in the aspect of this animal, for though he lifted on us grave and sagacious eyes, he scarcely seemed to see us, manifested neither pleasure nor disapproval, neither wagged his tail to give us welcome nor yawned to display his armament. He seemed a kind of dream-dog, a dog one sees without zeal, and sees again partly with the eye, but most in recollection.

27

Thus, however, we stood, stranger, horse, and dog, till a morose voice called somewhere from beyond, "Pilot, sir, come here, Pilot." Semi-dog or no, he knew his master. Whereupon, tying up my dejected Rosinante to a ring in the gateway, I followed boldly after "Pilot" into that sequestered garden.

Meanwhile, however, he had disappeared—down a thick green alley to the left, I supposed. So I went forward by a clearer path, and when I had advanced a few paces, met face to face a lady whose dark eyes seemed strangely familiar to me.

She was evidently a little disquieted at meeting a stranger so unceremoniously, but stood her ground like a small, black, fearless note of interrogation.

I explained at once, therefore, as best I could, how I came to be there: described my journey, my bewilderment, and how that I knew not into what country nor company fate had beguiled me, except that the one was beautiful, and the other in some delightful way familiar, and I begged her to tell me where I really was, and how far from home, and of whom I was now beseeching forgiveness.

Her thoughts followed my every word, passing upon her face like shadows on the sea. I have never seen a listener so completely still and so completely engrossed in listening. And when I had finished, she looked aside with a transient, half-sly smile, and glanced at me again covertly, so that I could not see herself for seeing her eyes; and she laughed lightly.

"It is indeed a strange journey," she replied. "But I fear I cannot in the least direct you. I have never ventured my own self beyond the woods, lest—I should penetrate too far. But you are tired and hungry. Will you please walk on a few steps till you come to a stone seat? My name is Rochester—Jane Rochester"—she glanced up between the hollies with a sigh that was all but laughter—"Jane Eyre, you know."

I went on as she had bidden, and seated myself before an old, white, many-windowed house, squatting, like an owl at noon, beneath its green covert. In a few minutes the great dog with dripping jowl passed almost like reality, and after him his mistress, and on her arm her master, Mr. Rochester.

There seemed a night of darkness in that scarred face, and stars unearthly bright. He peered dimly at me, leaning heavily on Jane's arm, his left hand plunged into the bosom of his coat. And when he was come near, he lifted his hat to me with a kind of Spanish gravity.

"Is this the gentleman, Jane?" he inquired.

"Yes, sir."

"He's young!" he muttered.

"For otherwise he would not be here," she replied.

"Was the gate bolted, then?" he asked.

"Mr. Rochester desires to know if you had the audacity, sir, to scale his garden wall," Jane said, turning sharply on me. "Shall I count the strawberries, sir?" she added over her shoulder.

"Jane, Jane!" he exclaimed testily. "I

have no wish to be uncivil, sir. We are not of the world—a mere dark satellite. I am dim; and suspicious of strangers, as this one treacherous eye should manifest. I'll but ask your name, sir—there are yet a few names left, once pleasing to my ear."

"My name is Brocken, sir—Henry Brocken," I answered.

"And—did you walk? Pah! there's the mystery! God knows how else you could have come, unless you are a modern Ganymede. Where then's your aquiline steed, sir? We have no neighbours here—none to stare, and pry, and prate, and slander."

I informed him that I was as ignorant as he what power had spirited me to his house, but that so far as obvious means went, my old horse was probably by this time fast asleep beside the green gate at which I had entered. Jane stood on tip-toe and whispered in his ear, and, nodding imperiously at him, withdrew into the house.

Complete silence fell between us after her departure. The woods stood dark and motionless in the yellow evening light. There was no sound of wind or water, no sound of voices or footsteps; only far away the clear, scarce-audible warbling of a sleepy bird.

"Well, sir," Mr. Rochester said suddenly, "I am bidden invite you to pass the night here. There are stranger inhabitants than Mr. and Mrs. Rochester in these regions you have by some means strayed into—wilder denizens, by much: for youth's seraphic finding. Not for mine, sir, I vow. Depart again in the morning, if you will: we shall neither of us be displeased by then to say farewell, I dare say. I do not seek company. My obscure shell is enough." I rose. "Sit down— sit down again, my dear sir; there's no mischief in the truth between two men of any world, I suppose, assuredly not of this. My wife will see to your comfort. There! hushie now, here he floats; sit still, sit still—I hear his wings. It is my 'Four Evangels,' sir!"

It was a sleek blackbird that had alighted and now set to singing on the topmost twig of a lofty pear-tree near by; and with his first note Jane reappeared. And while we listened, unstirring, to that rich, undaunted voice, I had good opportunity to observe her, and not, I think, without her knowledge, not even without her approval.

This, then, was the face that had returned wrath for wrath, remorse for remorse, passion for passion to that dark egotist Jane in the looking-glass. Yet who, thought I, could be else than beautiful with eyes that seemed to hide in fleeting cloud a flame as pure as amber? The arch simplicity of her gown, her small, narrow hands, the exquisite cleverness of mouth and chin, the lovely courage and sincerity of that yet-childish brow—it seemed even Mr. Rochester's "Four Evangels" out of his urgent rhetoric was summoning with reiterated persuasions, "Jane Eyre, Jane Eyre, Jane Eyre, Ja . . . ne!"

Light faded from the woods; a faint wind blew cold upon our faces. Jane took Mr. Rochester's hand and looked into his face.

She turned to me. "Will you come in, Mr. Brocken? I have seen that your horse is

made quite easy. He was fast asleep, poor
fellow, as you surmised; and, I think, dream-
ing; for when I proffered him a lump of
sugar, he thrust his nose into my face and
breathed as if I were a peck of corn. The
candles are lit, sir; supper is ready."

We went in slowly, and Jane bolted the
door. "But who it is that can be bolted out,"
she said, "I know not; though there's much to
bolt in. I have stood there, Mr. Brocken, on
darker nights as still as this, and have heard
what seemed to be the sea breaking, far away,
leagues upon leagues beyond the forests—the
gush forward, the protracted, heavy retreat
—listened till I could have wept to think that
it was only my own poor furious heart beat-
ing. You may imagine, then, I push the bolts
home."

"But why, Jane—why?" cried Mr.
Rochester incredulously. "Violent fancies,
child!"

"Why, sir, it was, I say, not the sea I heard,
but a trickling tide one icy tap might stay,
if it found but entry there."

"You talk wildly, Jane—wildly, wildly; the air's afloat with listeners; so it seems, so it seems. Had I but one clear lamp in this dark face!"

We sat down in the candle-lit twilight to supper. It was to me like the supper of a child, taken at peace in the clear beams, ere he descend into the shadow of sleep.

They sat, try as I would not to observe them, hand touching hand throughout the meal. But to me it was as if one might sit to eat before a great mountain ruffled with pines, and perpetually clamorous with torrents. All that Mr. Rochester said, every gesture, these were but the ghosts of words and movements. Behind them, gloomy, imperturbable, withdrawn, slumbered a strange, smouldering power. I began to see how very hotly Jane must love him, she who loved above all things storm, the winds of the equinox, the illimitable night-sky.

She begged him to take a little wine with me, and filled his glass till it burned like a ruby between their hands.

35

"It paints both our hands!" she cried, glancing up at him.

"Ay, Janet," he answered; "but where is yours?"

"And what goal will you make for when you leave us?" she inquired of me. *"Is* there anything else?" she added, lifting her slim eyebrows.

"I shall put trust in Chance," I replied, "which at least is steadfast in change. So long as it does not guide me back, I care not how far forward I go."

"You are right," she answered; "that is a puissant battlecry, here and hereafter."

Mr. Rochester rose hastily from his chair. "The candles irk me, Jane. I would like to be alone. Excuse me, sir." He left the room.

Jane lifted a dark curtain and beckoned me to bring the lights. She sat down before a little piano and desired me to sit beside her. And while she played, I know not what, but only it seemed old, well-remembered airs her mood suggested, she asked me many questions.

"And am I indeed only like that poor mad thing you thought Jane Eyre?" she said, "or did you read between?"

I answered that it was not her words, not even her thoughts, not even her poetry that was to me Jane Eyre.

"What then is left of me?" she inquired, stooping her eyes over the keys and smiling darkly. "Am I indeed so evanescent, a wintry wraith?"

"Well," I said, "Jane Eyre is left."

She pressed her lips together. "I see," she said brightly. "But then, was I not detestable too? so stubborn, so wilful, so demented, so —vain?"

"You were vain," I answered, "because——"

"Well?" she said, and the melody died out, and the lower voices of her music complained softly on.

"For a barrier," I answered.

"A barrier?" she cried.

"Why, yes," I said, "a barrier against cant, and flummery, and coldness, and pride, and

37

against—why, against your own vanity too."

"That's really very clever—penetrating," she said; "and I really desired to know, not because I did not know already, but to know I knew all. You are a perspicacious observer, Mr. Brocken; and to be that is to be alive in a world of the moribund. But then too how high one must soar at times; for one must ever condescend in order to observe faithfully. At any rate, to observe all one must range at an altitude above all."

"And so," I said, "you have taken your praise from me——"

"But you are a man, and I a woman: we look with differing eyes, each sex to the other, and perceive by contrast. Else—why, how else could you forgive my presumption? He sees me as an eagle sees the creeping tortoise. I see him as the moon the sun, never weary of gazing. I borrow his radiance to observe him by. But I weary you with my garrulous tongue. . . . Have you no plan at all in your journey? 'Tis not the dangers, but to me the endless restlessness of such a venture—that

'Oh, where shall wisdom be found?' . . . Will you not pause?—stay with us a few days to consider again this rash journey? To each his world: it is surely perilous to transgress its fixed boundaries."

"Who knows?" I cried, rather arrogantly perhaps. "The sorcery that lured me hither may carry me as lightly back. But I have tasted honey and covet the hive."

She glanced sidelong at me with that stealthy gravity that lay under all her lightness.

"That delicious Rosinante!" she exclaimed softly. . . . "And I really believe too *I* must be the honey—or is it Mr. Rochester? Ah! Mr. Brocken, they call it wasp-honey when it is so bitter that it blisters the lips." She talked on gaily, as if she had forgotten I was but a stranger until now. Yet none the less she presently perceived my eyes fixed ever and again upon the little brooch of faintest gold hair at her throat, and she flinched and paled, playing on in silence.

"Take the whole past," she continued

abruptly, "spread it out before you, with all its just defeats, all its broken faith, and over-weening hopes, its beauty, and fear, and love, and its loss—its loss; then turn and say: this, this only, this duller heart, these duller eyes, this contumacious spirit is all that is left—myself. Oh! who could wish to one so dear a destiny so dark?" She rose hastily from the piano. "Did I hear Mr. Rochester's step by the window?" she said.

I crossed the room and looked out into the night. The brightening moon hung golden in the dark clearness of the sky. Mr. Rochester stood motionless, Napoleonwise, beneath the black, unstirring foliage. And before I could turn, Jane had begun to sing:—

> You take my heart with tears;
> I battle uselessly;
> Reft of all hopes and doubts and fears,
>   Lie quietly.
>
> You veil my heart with cloud;
> Since faith is dim and blind,

I can but grope perplex'd and bow'd,
   Seek till I find.

  Yet bonds are life to me;
  How else could I perceive
The love in each wild artery
  That bids me live?

Jane's was not a rich voice, nor very sweet, and yet I fancied no other voice than this could plead and argue quite so clearly and with such nimble insistency—neither of bird, nor child, nor brook; because, I suppose, it was the voice of Jane Eyre, and all that was Jane's seemed Jane's only.

The music ceased, the accompaniment died away; but Mr. Rochester stood immobile yet —a little darker night in that much deeper. When I turned, Jane was gone from the room. I sat down, my face towards the still candles, as one who is awake, yet dreams on. The faint scent of the earth through the open window; the heavy, sombre furniture; the daintiness and the alertness in the many flowers and few womanly gew-gaws: these too I shall remember in a tranquillity that cannot change.

A sudden, trembling glimmer at the window lit the garden and, instantaneously, the distant hills; lit also the figures of Jane and Mr. Rochester beneath the trees. They entered the house, and once more Jane drew the bolts against that phantom fear. A tinge of scarlet stood in her cheeks, an added lustre in her eyes. They were strange lovers, these two—like frost upon a cypress tree; yet summer lay all around us.

I bade them good-night and ascended to the little room prepared for me. There was a great pincushion on the sprigged and portly toilet table, and I laboured till the constellations had changed beyond my window, in printing from a box of tiny pins upon that lavendered mound, *"Ave, Ave, atque Vale!"*

Far in the night a dreadful sound woke me. I rose and looked out of the window, and heard again, deep and reverberating, Pilot baying I know not what light minions of the moon. The Great Bear wheeled faintly clear in the dark zenith, but the borders of the east were grey as glass; and far away a fierce hound was answering from his echo-place in the gloom, as if the dread dog of Acheron kept post upon the hills.

A light tap woke me in the sunlight, and a lighter voice. Mr. Rochester took breakfast with us in a gloomy old dressing-room, moody and taciturn, unpacified by sleep. But Jane, whimsical and deft, had tied a yellow ribbon in the darkness of her hair.

Rosinante awaited me at the little green gate, eyeing forlornly the steep valley at her feet. And I rode on. The gate was shut on me; and Mr. Rochester again, perhaps, at his black ease.

I had jogged on, with that peculiar gravity age brings to equine hoofs, about a mile, when the buttress of a thick wall came into view abutting on the lane, and perched thereon what at first I deemed a coloured figment of the mist that festooned the branches and clung along the turf. But when I drew near I saw it was indeed a child, pink and gold and palest blue. And she raised changeling hands at me, and laughed and danced and chattered like the drops upon a waterfall; and clear as if a tiny bell had jingled I heard her cry.

And my heart smote me heavily since I had of my own courtesy not remembered Adèle.

Chapter Four

Cuckoo, jug-jug, pu-we, tu-witta-woo.
THOMAS NASH.

IT was yet early, and refreshing in the chequered shade. We plodded earnestly after our gaunt shadow in the dust, and ever downward, till at last we drew so near to the opposite steep that I could wellnigh count its pines.

It was about the hour when birds seek shade and leave but few among their fellows to sing, that at a stone's throw from the foot of the hill I came to where a faint bridle-path diverged. And since it was smooth with moss, and Rosinante haply tired of pebbles; since any but the direct road seems ever the more delectable, I too turned aside, and broke into the woods through which this path meandered.

Maybe it is because all woods are enchanted that the path seemed more than many miles long. Often, too, we loitered, or stood, head by head, to listen, or to watch what might be after all only wings, mere sunbeams. Shall I say, then, that it began to be thorny, and, where the thorns were, pale with roses, when at length the knitted boughs gradually drew asunder, and I looked down between twitching, hairy ears upon a glade so green and tranquil, I deemed it must be the Garden of the Hesperides?

And because there ran a very welcome brook of water through this glade, I left Rosinante to follow whithersoever a sweet tooth might dictate, and climbed down into the weedy coolness at the waterbrink.

I confess I laughed to see so puckered a face as mine in the clear blue of the flowing water. But I dipped my hands and my head into the cold shallows none the less pleasantly, and was casting about for a deeper pool where I might bathe unscorned of the noonday, when I heard a light laughter behind me, and, turning cautiously, perceived under the further shadow of the glade three ladies sitting.

Not even vanity could persuade me that they were laughing at anything more grotesque than myself, so, putting a bold face on matters so humiliating, I sauntered as carelessly and loftily as I dared in their direction. My courage seemed to abash them a little; they gathered back their petticoats like birds about to fly. But at hint of a titter, they all three began gaily laughing again till their eyes sparkled brighter than ever, and their cheeks seemed shadows of the roses above their heads.

"Ladies," I began gravely, "I have left my horse, that is very old and very thirsty, above in the wood. Is there any path I may discover by which she may reach the water without offence?"

"Is she very old?" said one.

"She is very old," I said.

"But is she very thirsty?" said another.

"She is perhaps very thirsty," I said.

" 'Perhaps'!" cried they all.

47

"Because, ladies," I replied, "being by nature of a timid tongue, and compelled to say something, and having nothing apt to say, I remembered my old Rosinante above in the wood."

They glanced each at each, and glanced again at me.

"But there is no path down that is not steep," said the fairest of the three.

"There never was a path, not even, we fear, for a traveller on foot," continued the second.

I waited in silence a moment. "Forgive me, then," I said; "I will offend no longer."

But this seemed far from their design.

"You see, being come," began the fairest again, "Julia thinks Fortune must have brought you. Are we not all between Fortune's finger and thumb?"

"If pinching is to prove anything," said the other.

"And Fortune is fickle, too," added Julia —"that's early wisdom; but not quite so fickle as you would wish to show her. Here

we have sat in these mortal glades ever since
our poor Herrick died. And here it seems
we are like to sit till he rises again. It is all
so—dubious. But since Electra has invited
you to rest awhile, will you not really rest?
There is shade as deep, and fruit to refresh
you, in a little arbour yonder. Perhaps even
Anthea will dip out of her weeping awhile
if she hears that . . . a poor old thirsty horse
is tethered in the woods."

They rose up together with a prolonged
rustling as of a peacock displaying his
plumes; and I found myself irretrievably
their captive.

Moreover, even if they were but sylphs
and fantasies of the morning, they were fan-
tasies lovely as even their master had por-
trayed; while the dells through which they
led me were green and deep and white and
golden with buds.

It was now, I suppose, about the middle
of the morning, yet though the sun was high,
his heat was that of dawn. Dawn lingered
in the shadows, as snow when winter is over

and gone, and dwelt among the sunbeams. Dew lay heavy on the grass, as the dainty heels of my captresses testified, yet they trod lightly upon daisies wide-open to the blue sky, while daffadowndillies stooped in a silence broken only by their laughter.

We came presently to a little stone summer-house or arbour, enclustered with leaves and flowers of ivy and convolvulus, wherein two great dishes of cherries stood and bowls of honeycomb and sillabub.

There we sat down; but they kept me close too in the midst of the arbour, where perhaps I was not so ill-content to be as I should like to profess. How then could I else than bob for cherries as often as I dared, and prove my wit to conceal my hunger?

"And now, Sir Traveller," said she of the sparkling eyes, named Dianeme, "since we have got you safe, tell us of all we have never heard or seen!"

"And oh! are we forgot?" cried Electra, laying a lip upon a cherry.

"There's not a poet in his teens but warbles

of you morn, noon, and night," I answered.
"There's not a lover mad, young, true, and
tender, but borrows your azure, and your
rubies, and your roses, and your stars, to deck
his sweetheart's name with."

"Boys perhaps," cried Julia softly, "but
men soon forget."

"Youth never," I replied.

"Why 'Youth'?" said Dianeme. "Herrick
was not always young."

"Ay, but all men *once* were young, please
God," I said, "and youth is the only 'once'
that's worth remembrance. Youth with the
heart of youth adores you, ladies; because,
when dreams come thick upon them, they
catch your flying laughter in the woods.
When the sun is sunk, and the stars kindle
in the sky, then your eyes haunt the twilight.
You come in dreams, and mock the waking.
You the mystery; you the bravery and dan-
ger; you the long-sought; you the never-won;
memories, hopes, songs ere the earth is mute.
You will always be loved, believe me, O
bright ladies, till youth fades, turns, and loves

no more." And I gazed amazed on cherries of such potency as these.

"But once, sir," said Julia timidly, "we were not only loved but *told* we were loved."

"Where is the pleasure else?" cried Dianeme.

"Besides," said Electra, "Anthea says if we might but find where Styx flows, one draught —my mere palmful—would be sweeter than all the poetry ever writ, save some."

"It is idle," cried Dianeme; "Herrick himself admired us most on paper."

"And ink makes a cross even of a kiss, that is very well known," said Julia.

"Ah!" said I, "all men have eyes; few see. Most men have tongues: there is but one Robin Herrick."

"I will tell you a secret," said Dianeme.

And as if a bird of the air had carried her voice, it seemed a hush fell on sky and greenery.

"We are but fairy-money all," she said. "An envy to see; but take us!—'tis all dry leaves in the hand. Herrick stole the honey, and the bees he killed. Blow never so softly, the tinder flames—and dies."

"I heard once," said Electra, with but a thought of pride, "that had I lived a little, little earlier, I might have been the Duchess of Malfi."

"I too, Flatterer," cried Julia, "I too—Desdemona slain by a blackamoor. To some it is the cold hills and the valleys 'green and sad,' and the sea-birds' wailing," she continued in a low, strange voice, "and to some the glens of heather, and the mountain-brooks, and the rowans. But, come to an end, what are we all? This man's eyes will tell ye! I would give white and red, nectar and snow and roses, and all the similes that ever were for——"

"For what?" said I.

"I think, for Robin Herrick," she said.

It was a lamentable confession, for that said, gravity fled away; and Electra fetched out a lute from a low cupboard in the arbour, and while she played, Julia sang to a sober little melody I seemed to know of old:—

53

Henry Brocken

Sighs have no skill
To wake from sleep
Love once too wild, too deep.

Gaze if thou will,
Thou canst not harm
Eyes shut to subtle charm.

Oh! 'tis my silence
Shows thee false,
Should I be silent else?

Haste thou then by!
Shine not thy face
On mine, and love's disgrace!

Whereat Dianeme lifted on me so naïve an afflicted face I must needs beseech another song, despite my drowsy lids. Wherefore I heard, far away as it were, the plucking of the strings, and a voice betwixt dream and wake sing:—

All sweet flowers
Wither ever,
Gathered fresh

54

Or gathered never;
But to live when love is gone!—
Grieve, grieve, lute, sadly on!

All I had—
   'Twas all thou gav'st me;
That foregone,
   Ah! what can save me?
If the exòrcised spirit fly,
Nought is left to love me by.

Take thy stars,
   My tears then leave me;
Thine my bliss,
   As thine to grieve me;
Take . . . . .

For then, so insidious was the music, and not quite of this earth the voice, my senses altogether forsook me, and I fell asleep.

Would that I could remember much else! But I confess it is the heart remembers, not the poor pestered brain that has so many thoughts and but one troubled thinker. Indeed, were I now to be asked—Were the fingers cold of these bright ladies? Were their

eyes blue, or hazel, or brown? Or, haply,
were Dianeme's that incomparable, dark,
sparkling grey? Wore Julia azure, and
Electra white? And was that our poet wrote
our poet's only, or truly theirs, and so even
more lovely?—I fear I could not tell.

I fell asleep; and when I awoke no lute
was sounding. I was alone; and the arbour
a little house of gloom on the borders of
evening. I caught up yet one more handful
of cherries, and stumbled out, heavy and dim,
into a pale-green firmament of buds and
glow-worms, to seek the poor Rosinante I
had so heedlessly deserted.

But I was gone but a little way when I
was brought suddenly to a standstill by an-
other sound that in the hush of the garden, in
the bright languor after sleep, went to my
heart: it was as if a child were crying.

I pushed through a thick and aromatic
clump of myrtles, and peering between the
narrow leaves, perceived the cold, bright face
of a little marble god beneath willows; and,
seated upon a starry bank near by, one whom

by the serpentry of her hair and the shadow of her lips I knew to be Anthea.

"Why are you weeping?" I said.

"I was imitating a little brook," she said.

"It is late; the bat is up; yet you are alone," I said.

"Pan will protect me," she said.

"And nought else?"

She turned her face away. "None," she said. "I live among shadows. There was a world, I dreamed, where autumn follows summer, and after autumn, winter. Here it is always June, despite us both."

"What, then, would you have?" I said.

"Ask him," she replied.

But the little god, looking sidelong, was mute in his grey regard.

"Why do you not run away? What keeps you here?"

"You ask many questions, stranger! Who can escape? To live is to remember. To die—oh, who would forget! Even had I been weeping, and not merely mocking time away, would my tears be of Lethe at my

Henry Brocken

mouth's corners? No," said Anthea, "why
feign and lie? All I am is but a memory
lovely with regret."

She rose, and the myrtles concealed her
from me. And I, in the midst of the dusk
where the tiny torches burned sadly—I turned
to the sightless eyes of that smiling god.

What he knew, being blind, yet smiling, I
seemed to know then. But that also I have
forgotten.

I whistled softly and clearly into the air,
and a querulous voice answered me from afar
—the voice of a grasshopper—Rosinante's.

Chapter Five

How should I your true love know
From another one?

WILLIAM SHAKESPEARE.

BUT even then she was difficult finding, so cunningly had ivy and blackberry and bindweed woven snares for the trespasser's foot.

But at last—not far from where we had parted—I found her, a pillar of smoke in the first shining of the moon. She turned large, smouldering eyes on me, her mane in elf locks, her flanks heaving and wet, her fore-lock frizzed like a colt's. Yet she showed only pleasure at seeing me, and so evident a desire to unburden the day's history, that I almost wished I might be Balaam awhile, and she—Dapple!

It would be idle to attempt to ride through these thick, glimmering brakes. The darkness was astir. And as the moon above the valley brightened, casting pale beams upon the folded roses and drooping branches, if populous dream did not deceive me, a tiny multitude was afoot in the undergrowth— small horns winding, wee tapers burning.

Presently as with Rosinante's nose at my shoulder we pushed slowly forward, a nightingale burst close against my ear into so passionate a descant I thought I should be gooseflesh to the end of my days.

The heedless tumult of her song seemed to give courage to sounds and voices much fainter. Soon a lovelit rival in some distant thicket broke into song, and far and near their voices echoed above the elfin din of timbrel and fife and hunting-horn. I began to wish the moon away that dazzled my eyes, yet could not muffle my ears.

In the heavy-laden boughs dim lanterns burned. There, indeed, when we dipped into the deeper umbrage of some loftier tree, I espied the pattering hosts—creatures my Dianeme might have threaded for a bangle, yet breeched and armed and fiercely martial.

Down, too, in a watery dell of hart's-tongue, around the root of a swelling fungus, a lovely company floated of an insubstantiality subtile as taper-smoke, and of a beauty as remote as the babes in children's eyes.

We passed unheeded. Four bearded hoofs rose and fell upon the moss with all the circumspection snorting Rosinante could compass. But one might as well go snaring moonbeams as dream to crush such airy beings. Ever and again a gossamer company would soar like a spider on his magic thread, and float with a whisper of remotest music past my ear; or some bolder pygmy, out of the leaves we brushed in passing, skip suddenly across the rusty amphitheatre of my saddle into the further covert.

So we wandered on, baffled and confused, through a hundred pathless glens and dells till already gold had begun to dim the swelling moon's bright silver, and by the freshness and added sweetness of the air it seemed dawn must be near, when, on a sudden, a harsh, preposterous voice broke on my ear, and such a see-saw peal of laughter as I have never tittered in sheer fellowship with before, or since. We stood listening, and the voice broke out again.

"Tittany—nay, Tittany, you'll crack my sides with laughing. Have again at you! love your master and you'll wax nimble. Bottom will learn you all. Trust Time and Bottom; though in sooth your weeny Majesty is something less than natural. Drive thy straw deeper, Mounsieur Mustardseed! There squats a pestilent sweet notion in that chamber could spellican but set him capering. Prithee, your mousemilk hand on this smooth brow, mistress! Your nectar throbbeth like a blacksmith's anvil. Master Moth, draw you these bristling lashes down, they mirk the stars and call yon nothing, Quince, to mind —a vain, official knave, in and out, to and fro, play or pleasure; and old Sam Snout, the wanton! Lad's days and all—'twas life, Tittany; and 1 was ever foremost. They'd bob and crook to me like spaniels at a trencher.

Mine was the prettiest conceit, this way, that way, past all unravelling till envy stretched mine ears. Now I'm old dreams. Gone all men's joy, your worships, since Bully Bottom took to moonshine. Where floats your babe's-hand now, Dame Lovepip?"

There he lolled, immortal Bottom, propped on a bed of asphodel and moly that seemed to curd the moonshine; and at his side, Titania, slim and scarlet, and shimmering like a bride-cake. The sky was dark above the tapering trees, but here in the secret woods light seemed to cling in flake and scarf. And it so chanced as our two noses leaned forward into his retreat that Bottom's head lolled back upon its pillow, and his bright, simple eyes stared deep into our own.

"Save me, ye shapes of nought," he bellowed, "no more, no more, for love's sake. I begin to see what men call red Beelzebub, and that's an end to all true fellowship. Whiffle your tufted bee's wing, Signior Cobweb, I beseech you—a little fiery devil with four eyes floats in my brain, and flame's a frisky bedfellow. Avaunt! avaunt ye! Would now my true friend Bottom, the weaver, were at my side. His was a courage to make princes great. Prithee, Queen Tittany, no more such cozening possets!"

I drew Rosinante back into the leaves.

"Droop now thy honeyed lids, my dearest love!" I heard a clear voice answer. "There's nought can harm thee in these silvered woods: no bird that pipes but love incites his throat, and never a dewdrop wells but whispers peace!"

"Ay, ay, 'tis very well, you have a gift, you have a gift. Tittany's for twisting words into sugarsticks. But la, there, what wots your trickling whey of that coal-piffling Prince of Flies! I'm Bottom the weaver, I am. He knows not his mother's ring-finger that knows not Nick Bottom. Back, back, ye jigging dreams! 'Tis Puckling nods. Ha' done, ha' done—there's no sweet sanity in an asshead more if I quaff their elvish . . . Out now . . . Ha' done, I say!"

Then indeed he slumbered truly, this engarlanded weaver, his lids concealing all bright speculation, his jowl of vanity (foe of the Philistine) at peace: and I might gaze unperceived. The moon filled his mossy cubicle with her untrembling beams, streamed upon blossoms sweet and heavy as Absalom's hair, while tiny plumes wafted into the night the scent of thyme and meadow-sweet.

I know not how long they would have kept me prisoner with their illusive music. I dared not move, scarce wink; for much as immortality may mollify hairiness, I had no wish to live too frank.

How, also, would this weaver who slumbered so cacophonously welcome a rival to his realms? I say I sat still, like Echo in the woods when none is calling; like too, I grant, one who ached not a little after jolts and jars and the phantasmal mists of this engendering air. But none stirred, nor went, nor came. So resting my hands cautiously on a little witch's guild of toadstools that squatted cold in shade, I lifted myself softly and stood alert.

And in a while out of that numerous company stepped one whom by his primrose face and mien I took to be Mounsieur Mustard-seed, and I followed after him.

Chapter Six

Care-charming Sleep . . .
. . . sweetly thyself dispose
On this afflicted prince!

JOHN FLETCHER.

AWAY with a blink of his queer green eye over his shoulder he sauntered by a devious path out of the dell. Forgetful of thorn and brier, trickery and wantonness, we clambered down after him, out of the moonlight, into a dark, clear alley, soundless and solitary amid these enchanted woods.

As I have already said, another air than that of night was abroad in the green-grey shadows of the woods. Yet between the lofty and heavy-hooded pines scarce a beam of dawn pierced downward.

Wider swept the avenue, but ever dusky and utterly silent. Deeper moss couched here; unfallen moondrops glistened; mistletoe

67

palely sprouted from the gnarled boughs. Nor could I discern, though I searched close enough, elder or ash tree or bitter rue. We journeyed softly on till I lost all count of time, lost, too, all guidance; for as a flower falls had vanished Mustardseed.

Far away and ever increasing in volume I heard the trembling crash of some great water falling. What narrow isles of sky were visible between the branches lay sunless and still. Yet already, on a mantled pool we journeyed softly by, the waterlily was unfolding, the swan afloat in beauty.

In a dim, still light we at last slowly descended out of the darker glade into a garden of gray terraces and flowerless walks. Even Rosinante seemed perturbed by the stillness and solitude of this wild garden. She trod with cautious foot and peering eye the green, rainworn paths, that led us down presently to where beneath the vault of its trees a river flowed.

Surely I could not be mistaken that here a voice was singing as if out of the black water-

deeps, so clear and hollow were the notes. I
burst through the knotted stalks of the ivy,
and stooping like some poor travesty of Nar-
cissus, with shaded face pierced down deep—
deep into eyes not my own, but violet and un-
endurable and strange—eyes of the living
water-sprite drawing my wits from me, still-
ing my heart, till I was very near plunging
into that crystal oblivion, to be fishes ever
after.

But my fingers still grasped my friend's
kind elf-locks, and her goose-nose brooded be-
side mine upon that water of undivulged de-
light. Out of the restless silence of the stream
floated this long-drawn singing:—

Pilgrim, forget; in this dark tide
Sinks the salt tear to peace at last;
Here undeluding dreams abide,
   All sorrow past.

Nods the wild ivy on her stem;
The voiceless bird broods on the bough;
The silence and the song of them
   Untroubled now.

69

Henry Brocken

Free the poor captive's flutterings,
That struggles in thy tired eyes,
Solace its discontented wings,
    Quiet its cries!

Knells now the dewdrop to its fall,
The sad wind sleeps no more to rove;
Rest, for my arms ambrosial
    Ache for thy love!

I cannot think how one so meekened with hunger as I, resisted that water-troubled hair, eyes that yet haunt me, that heart-alluring voice.

"No, no," I said faintly, and the words of Anthea came unbidden to mind, "to sleep—oh! who would forget? You plead merely with some old dream of me—not *all* me, you know. Gold is but witchcraft. And as for sorrow—spread me a magical table in this nettle-garden, I'll leave all melancholy!"

I must indeed have been exhausted to chop logic with a water-witch. As well argue with minnows, entreat the rustling of ivy-leaves. It was Rosinante, wearying, I suppose, of the reflection of her own mild countenance, that drew me back from dream and disaster. She turned with arched neck seeking a more wholesome pasture than these deep mosses.

Leaving her then to her own devices, and yet hearkening after the voice of the charmer, I came out again into the garden, and perceived before me a dark palace with one lofty tower.

It seemed strange I had not seen the tower at my first coming into this wilderness. It stood with clustered summit and stooping gargoyles, appealing as it were to fear, in utter silence.

Though I knew it must be day, there was scarcely more than a green twilight around me, ever deepening, until at last I could but dimly discern the upper windows of the palace, and all sound waned but the roar of distant falling water.

Then it was I found that I was not alone in the garden. Two little leaden children stood in an attitude of listening on either side of the carved porch of the palace, and between them a figure that seemed to be watching me intently.

I looked and looked again—saw the green-grey folds, the tawny locks, the mistletoe, the unearthly eyes of this unstirring figure, yet, when I advanced but one strenuous pace, saw nought—only the little leaden boys and the porch between them.

These childish listeners, the straggling briers, the impenetrable thickets, the emerald gloaming, the marble stillness of the lofty lichenous tower: I took courage. Could such things be in else than Elfland? And she who out of beauty and being vanishes and eludes, what else could she be than one of Elfland's denizens from whom a light and credulous heart need fear nothing?

I trod like a shadow where the phantom had stood and opened the unused door. I was about to pass into the deeper gloom of the house when a hound appeared and stood regarding me with shining eyes in the faint gloaming. He was presently joined by one as light-footed, but milk-white and slimmer,

and both turned their heads as if in question
of their master, who had followed close be-
hind them.

This personage, because of the gloom, or
the better to observe the intruder on his soli-
tude, carried a lantern, whose beams were re-
flected upon himself, attired as he was from
head to foot in the palest primrose, but with
a countenance yet paler.

There was no hint of enmity or alarm or
astonishment in the colourless eyes that were
fixed composedly on mine, nothing but cour-
tesy in his low voice.

"Back, Safte!—back, Sallow!" he cried
softly to his hounds; "is this your civility?
Indeed, sir," he continued to me, "it was all
I could do to dissuade the creatures from
giving tongue when you first appeared on
the terrace of my solitary gardens. I heard
too the water-sprite: she only sings when foot-
steps stray upon the banks." He smiled
wanly, and his nose seemed even sharper in
his pale face, and his yellow hair leaner about
his shoulders. "I feared her voice might

prove too persuasive, and deprive me of the first strange face I have seen these many decades gone."

I bowed and murmured an apology for my intrusion, just as I might perhaps to some apparition of nightmare that overstayed its welcome.

"I beseech you, sir," he replied, "say no more! It may be I deemed you at first a visitor perchance even more welcome—if it be possible, . . . yet I know not that either. My name is Ennui,"—he smiled again— "Prince Ennui. You have, perchance, heard somewhere our sad story. This is the perpetual silence wherein lies that once-happy princess, my dear sister, Sleeping Beauty."

His voice seemed but an echo amongst the walls and arches of this old house, and he spoke with a suave enunciation as if in an unfamiliar tongue.

I replied that I had read the ever-lovely story of Sleeping Beauty, indeed knew it by heart, and assured him modestly that I had not the least doubt of a happy ending—"that is, if the author be the least authority."

He narrowed his lids. "It is a tradition," he replied; "meanwhile, the thickets broaden."

Whereupon I begged him to explain how it chanced that among that festive and animated company I had read of, he alone had resisted the wicked godmother's spell.

He smiled distantly, and bowed me into the garden.

"That is a simple thing," he said.

Yet for the life of me I could not but doubt all he told me. He who could pass spring on to spring, summer on to summer, in the company of beasts so sly and silent, so alert and fleet as these hounds of his, could not be quite the amiable prince he feigned to be. I began to wish myself in homelier places.

It seems that on the morning of the fatal spindle, he had gone coursing, with his Safte and Sallow and his horse named Twilight, and after wearying and heating himself at

75

the sport, a little after noon, leaving his attendants, had set out to return to the palace alone. But allured by the cool seclusion of a "lattice-arbour" in his path, he had gone in, and then and there, Twilight beneath the willows, his hounds at his feet, had fallen asleep.

Undisturbed, dreamless, "the unseemly hours sped light of foot." He awoke again, between sunset and dark; the owl astir; "the silver gnats yet netting the shadows," and so returned to the palace.

But the spell had fallen—king and courtier, queen and lady and page and scullion, hawk and hound, slept a sleep past waking—"while I roamed, and roam yet, in a solitary watch beyond all sleeping. Wherefore, sir, I only of the most hospitable house in these lands am awake to bid you welcome. But as for that, a few dwindling and harsh fruits in my orchards, and the cold river water that my dogs lap with me, are all that is left to offer you. For I who never sleep am never hungry, and they who never wake—I presume—never thirst. Would, sir, it were otherwise! After such long silence, then, conceive how strangely falls your voice on ears that have heard only wings fluttering, dismal water-songs, and the yelp and quarrel and night-voice of unseen hosts in the forests."

He glanced at me with a mild austerity and again lowered his eyes. I cannot now but wonder how the rhythm of a voice so soft, so monotonous, could give such pleasure to the ear. I almost doubted my own eyes when I looked upon his yellow, on that unmoved, sad, mad, pale face.

I had no doubt of his dogs, however, and walked scarcely at ease beside him, while they, shadow-footed, closely followed us at heel.

"Prince Ennui" conducted me with shining lantern into a dense orchard thickly undergrown, marvellously green, with a small, hard fruit upon its branches, shaped like a medlar, of a crisp, sweet odour and, despite its hardness, a delicious taste. The interwoven twigs of the stooping trees were thickly nested; a veritable ·wilderness of moonlight and starry flowers ran all to seed amid the nettles and nightshade of this green silence. And while I ate—for I was hungry enough— Prince Ennui stood, his hand on Sallow's muzzle, lightly thridding the dusky labyrinths of the orchard with his faint green eyes.

Mine, too, were not less busy, but rather with its lord than with his orchard. And the strange thought entered my mind, Was he in very deed the incarnation of this solitude, this silence, this lawless abundance? Somewhere, in the green heats of summer, had he come forth, taken shape, exalted himself? What but vegetable ichor coursed through veins transparent as his? What but the swarming mysteries of these thick woods lurked in his brain? As for his hounds, theirs was the same stealth, the same symmetry, the same cold, secret unhumanity as his. Creatures begotten of moonlight on silence they seemed to me, with instincts past my workaday wits to conceive.

And Rosinante! I laughed softly to think

of her staid bones beside the phantom creature this prince had called up to me at mention of Twilight.

I ate because I was ravenously hungry, but also because, while eating, I was better at my ease.

Suddenly out of the stillness, like an arrow, Safte was gone; and far away beneath the motionless leaves a faint voice rang dwindling into silence. I shuddered at my probable fate.

Prince Ennui glanced lightly. "When the magic horn at last resounds," he said, "how strange a flight it will be! These thorny briers encroach ever nearer on my palace walls. I am a captive ever less at ease. Summer by summer the sun rises shorn yet closer of his beams, and now the lingering transit of the moon is but from one wood by an arrow crystal arch to another. They will have me yet, sir. How weary will the sleepy ones be of my uneasy footfall!"

And even as Safte slipped softly back to his watching mate, the patter and shrill menace of voices behind him hinted not all was concord between these hidden multitudes and their unseemly prince.

The master-stars shone earlier here; already sparkling above the tower was a canopy of clearest darkness spread, while the leafy fringes of the sky glowed yet with changing fires.

We returned to the lawns before the palace porch, and, with his lantern in his hand, the Prince signed to me to go in. I was not a little curious to view that enchanted household of which I had read so often and with so much delight as a child.

In the banqueting-hall only the matted windows were visible in the lofty walls. Prince Ennui held his lantern on high, and by its flame, and the faint light that flowed in from above, I could presently see, distinct in gloom, as many sleepers as even Night could desire.

Here they reclined just as sorcerous sleep had overtaken them. But how dimmed, how fallen! For Time that could not change the sleeper had changed with quiet skill all else.

Tarnished, dusty, withered, overtaken, yellowed and confounded lay banquet and cloth-of-gold, flagon, cup, fine linen, table and stool. But in all the ruin, like buds of springtime in a bare wood, or jewels in ashes, slumbered youth and beauty and bravery and delight.

I lifted my eyes to the King. The gold of his divinity was fallen, his splendour quenched; but life's dark scrutiny from his face was gone. He made no stir at our light, slumbered untreasoned on. The lids of his Queen were lightlier sealed, only withheld beauty as a cloud the sky it hides. His courtiers flattered more elusively, being sincerely mute, and only a little red dust was all the wine left.

I seemed to hear their laughter clearer now that the jest was forgotten, and to admire better the pomp, and the mirth, and the grace, and the vanity, now that time had so far travelled from this little tumult once their triumph.

In a kind of furtive bravado, I paced the

length of the long, thronged tables. Here
sat a little prince that captivated me, dipping
his fingers into his cup with a sidelong glance
at his mother. There a high officer, I know
not how magnificent and urgent when awake,
slumbered with eyes wide open above his dis-
couraged moustaches.

Simply for vanity of being awake in such
a sleepy company, I strutted conceitedly to
and fro. I bent deftly and pilfered a little
cockled cherry from between the very finger-
tips of her whose heart was doubtless like
its—quite hard. And the bright lips never
said a word. I sat down, rather clownishly
I felt, beside an aged and simpering chancel-
lor that once had seemed wise, but now
seemed innocent, nibbling a biscuit crisp as
scandal. For after all the horn *would* sound.
Childhood had been quite sure of that—
needed not even the author's testimony. They
were alert to rise, scattering all dust, victors
over Time and outrageous Fortune.

Almost with a cry of apprehension I per-
ceived again the solitary Prince. But he

merely smiled faintly. "You see, sir," he said, "how weary must a guardianship be of them who never tire. The snow falls, and the bright light falls on all these faces; yet not even my Lady Melancholy stirs a dark lid. And all these dog-days——" He glanced at his motionless hounds. They raised languidly their narrow heads, whimpering softly, as if beseeching of their master that long-delayed supper—haplessly me. "No, no, sirs," said the Prince, as if he had read their desire as easily as he whom it so much concerned. "Guard, guard, and hearken. This gentleman is not the Prince we await, Sallow; not the Prince, Safte! And now, sir,"—he turned again to me—"there is yet one other sleeper—she who hath brought so much quietude on a festive house."

We climbed the staircase where dim light lay so invitingly, and came presently to a little darker chamber. Green, blunt things had pushed and burst through the casement. The air smelled faintly-sour of brier, and was as still as boughs of snow. There the not-unhappy Princess reclined before a looking-glass, whither I suppose she had run to view her own alarm when the sharp needle pierced her thumb. All alarm was stilled now on her face. She, one might think, of all that company of the sleepy, was the only one that dreamed. Her youthful lips lay a little asunder; the heavy beauty of her hair was parted on her forehead; her childish hands sidled together like leverets in her lap. "Why!" I cried aloud, almost involuntarily, "she breathes!"

And at sound of my voice the hounds leapt back; and, on a traveller's oath, I verily believe, once, and how swiftly, and how fearfully and brightly, those childish lids unsealed their light as of lilac that lay behind, glanced briefly, fleetingly, on one who had ventured so far, and fell again to rest.

"And when," I cried harshly, "when will that laggard burst through this age-long silence? Here's dust enough for all to see. And all this ruin, this inhospitable peace!"

Prince Ennui glanced strangely at me.

"I assure you, O suddenly enkindled," he said in his suave, monotonous voice, "it is not for *my* indifference he does not come. I would willingly sleep; these—my dear sister, all these old fineries and love-jinglers would as fain wake." He turned away his treacherous eyes from me. "Maybe the Lorelei hath snared him! . . ." he said, smiling.

I relished not at all the thought of sleeping in this mansion of sleep. Yet it seemed politic to refrain from giving offence to fangs apparently so eager to take it. Accordingly I followed this Ennui to a loftier chamber yet that he suggested for me.

Once there, however, and his soft footfall passed away, I looked about me, first to find a means for keeping trespassers from coming in, and next to find a means for getting myself out.

It was a long and arduous, but not a perilous, descent from the window by the thick-grown greenery that cumbered the walls. But I determined to wait awhile before venturing—wait, too, till I could see plainly where Rosinante had made her night-quarters. By good fortune I discovered her beneath the greenish moon that hung amid mist above the forest, stretching a disconsolate neck at the waterside as if in search of the Lorelei.

When, as it seemed to me, it must be nearing dawn, though how the hours flitted so swiftly passed my comprehension, I very cautiously climbed out of my narrow window and descended slowly to the lawns beneath. My foot had scarcely touched ground when ringing and menacing from some dark gallery of the palace above me broke out a distant baying.

Nothing shall persuade me to tell how fast I ran; how feverishly I haled poor Rosinante out of sleep, and pushed her down into the deeps of that coal-black stream; with what agility I clambered into the saddle.

Yet I could not help commiserating the while the faithful soul who floated beneath me. The stream was swift but noiseless, the water rather rare than cold, yet, despite all the philosophy beaming out of her maidenly eyes across the smooth surface of the tide, Rosinante must have preferred from the bottom of her heart dry land.

I, too, momentarily, when I discovered that we were speedily approaching the roaring fall whose reverberations I had heard long since.

Out of the emerald twilight we floated from beneath the overarching thickets. Pale beams were striking from the risen sun upon the gliding surface, and dwelt in splendour where danger sat charioted beneath a palely gorgeous bow. Yet I doubt if ever mortal man swept on to defeat at last so rapturously as I.

The gloomier trees had now withdrawn from the banks of the river. A pale morning sky over-canopied the shimmering forests. Here rose the solitary tower where Echo tarried for the Hornblower. And straight before us, across that level floor, beyond a tremulous cloud of foam and light and colour, lurked the unseen, the unimaginable, the ever-dreamed-of, Death.

Heedless of Lorelei, heedless of all save the

beauty and terror and glory in which they rode, down swept snorting ship and master to doom.

The crystal water jargoned past my saddle. Sky, earth, and tower, like the panorama of a dream, wheeled around me. Light blinded me; clamour deafened me; foam and the pure wave and cold darkness whelmed over me. We surged, paused, gazed, nodded, crashed: —and so an end to Ennui.

Chapter Seven

He loves to talk with marineres
That come from a far countree.
                SAMUEL TAYLOR COLERIDGE.

HOW long my body was the sport of that foaming water I cannot tell. But when I again opened my eyes, I found, first, that the sun was shining dazzling clear high above me, and, next, that the delightful noise of running water babbled close against my ear. I lay upon a strip of warm sward by the river's brink. Near by me grew some rank-smelling waterside plant, and overhead the air seemed peopled with larks.

I crawled, confused and aching, to the water, and dipped my head and hands into the cold rills. This soon refreshed me, for the sun had, it would seem, long been dwelling on that passive corse of mine by the waterside and had parched it to the skin.

But it was some little while yet before my

mind returned fully to what had passed, and so to my loss.

I sat looking at the grey, noisy water, almost incredulous that Rosinante could be gone. It might be that the same hand as must have drawn myself from drowning had snatched her bridle also out of Fate's grasp. Perhaps even now she was seeking her master by the greener pasture of the wide plains around me. Perhaps the far-off sea was her green sepulchre. But many waters cannot quench love. I faced, friendless and discomfited, a region as strange to me as the further side of the moon.

Without more ado I rose, shook myself, and sadly began to go forward. But I had taken only a few steps along the banks of the stream—for here was fresh water, at least —when a sound like distant thunder rolled over these flat, green lands towards me, increasing steadily in volume.

I stood, lost in wonder, and presently, at the distance, perhaps, of a little less than a mile, descried an innumerable herd of horses streaming across these level pastures, and at the extremity, it seemed, of a wide ellipse, that had brought them near, and now was galloping them away.

My heart beat a little faster at this extraordinary spectacle. And while I stood in uncertainty gazing after the retreating concourse, I perceived a figure running towards me, lifting his hands and crying out in a voice sonorous and inhuman. He was of a stature much above my own, yet so gross in shape and immense of head he seemed at first almost dwarfish. He came to a stand twenty paces or so from me, on the ridge of a gentle inclination, and gazed down on me with wild, bright eyes. Even at this distance I could perceive the almost colourless lustre of his eyes beneath his thick locks of yellow hair. When he had taken his fill of me, he lifted his head again and cried out to me a few words of what certainly might be English, but was neither intelligible nor reassuring.

I stood my ground and stared him in the face, till I could see nothing but wind-blown yellow, and strange, brutal eyes. Then he advanced a little nearer. Whereupon I also raised my hand with a gesture like his own, and demanded loudly where I was, what was this place, and who was he. His very ears pricked forward, he listened so intently. He came nearer yet, then stayed, tossed his head into the air, whirled the long leather thong he carried above his head, and, signing to me to follow, set off with so swift and easy a stride that it would soon have carried him out of sight, had he not turned and perceived how slowly I could follow him.

He slackened his pace then, and, thus running, we came in sight at length of what appeared to be a vast wooden shed, or barn, with one rude chimney, and surrounded by a thick fence, or stockade, many feet high and apparently of immense strength and stability.

In the gateway of this fence stood the master of these solitudes, his eyes fixed strangely on my coming with an intense, I had almost said incredulous, interest. Nor did he cease so to regard me, while the creature that had conducted me thither, told, I suppose, where he had found me, and poured out with childish zeal his own amazement and delight. By this time, too, his voice had begun to lose its first strangeness, and to take a meaning for me. And I was presently fully persuaded he spoke a kind of English, and that not unpleasingly, with a liquid, shrill, voluminous ease. His master listened patiently awhile, but at last bade his servant be silent, and himself addressed me.

"I am informed, Yahoo," he said with peculiar deliberation, "that you have been borne down into my meadows by the river, and fetched out thence by my servant. Be aware, then, that all these lands from horizon to horizon are mine and my people's. I desire no tidings of what follies may be beyond my boundaries, no aid, and no amity. I admit no trespasser here and will bear with none. It appears, however, that your life has passed beyond your own keeping: I may not, therefore, refuse you shelter and food, and to have you conducted in safety beyond my borders.

93

Have the courtesy, then, to keep within shelter of these walls till the night be over. Else"—he gazed out across the verdant undulations—"else, Yahoo, I have no power to protect you."

He turned once more, and regarded me with a lofty yet tender recognition, as if, little though his speech might profess it, he very keenly desired my safety.

He then stepped aside and rather sharply bade me enter the gate before him. I tried to show none of the mistrust I felt at passing out of these open lands into this repellent yard. I glanced at the shock-haired creature, alert, half-human, beside me; across the limitless savannah around me, echoing yet, it seemed, with the rumour of innumerable hoofs; and bowing, as it were, to odds, I went in.

On the other hand, I felt my host had been frank with me. If this was indeed the same Lemuel Gulliver whose repute my infancy had prized so well, I need have no fear of blood and treachery at his hands, however primitive and disgusting his household, or distorted his intellect might be. He who had proved no tyrant in Lilliput, nor quailed before the enormities of Brobdingnag, might abhor the sight of me; he would not play me false.

His servant, or whatsoever else he might be, I considered not quite so calmly. Yet even in *his* broad countenance dwelt a something like bright honesty, less malice than simplicity.

Wherefore, I say, I ordered down my cowardice, and, looking both of them as squarely in the face as I knew how, passed out of the open into the appalling yard of this wooden house.

I say "appalling," but without much reason. Perhaps it was the unseemly hugeness of its balks, the foul piles of skins, the mounds of refuse that lay about within; perhaps the all-pervading beastly stench, the bareness and filthiness under so glassy-clear and fierce a sun that revolted me. All man's seemliness and affection for the natural things of earth

95

were absent. Here was only a brutal and bald order, as of an intelligence like that of the yellow-locked, swift-footed creature behind me. Perhaps also it was the mere unfamiliarity of much I saw there that estranged me. All lay in neglect, cracked and marred with rough usage—coarse strands of a kind of rope, strips of hide, gaping tubs, a huge and rusty brazier, and in one corner a great cage, many feet square and surmounted with an iron ring.

I know not. I almost desired Sallow at my side, and would to heaven Rosinante's nose lay in my palm.

Within the house a wood-fire burned in the sun, its smoke ascending to the roof, and flowing thence through a rude chimney. A pot steamed over the fire, burdening the air with a savour at first somewhat faint and disgusting—perhaps because it was merely strange to me. The walls of this lofty room were of rough, substantial timber, bare and weatherproof; the floor was of the colour of earth, seemingly earth itself. A few rude stools, a bench, and a four-legged table stood beside the unshuttered window. And from this stretched the beauteous green of the grass-land or prairie beyond the stockade.

The house, then, was built on the summit of a gentle mound, and doubtless commanded from its upper window the extreme reaches of this sea of verdure.

I sat down where Mr. Gulliver directed me, and was not displeased with the warmth of the fire, despite the sun. I was cold after that long, watery lullaby, and cold too with exhaustion after running so far at the heels of the creature who had found me. And I dwelt in a kind of dream on the transparent flames, and watched vacantly the seething pot, and smelt, till slowly appetite returned, the smoke of the stuff that bubbled beneath its lid.

Mr. Gulliver himself brought me my platter of this pottage, and though it tasted of nothing in my experience—a kind of sweet, cloying meat—I was so tired of the fruits to which enterprise had as yet condemned me, I ate of it hungrily and heartily. Yet not so

97

fast as that the young "Gulliver" had not fin-
ished his before me, and sat at length watch-
ing every mouthful I took from beneath his
sun-enticing thatch of hair. Ever and again
he would toss up his chin with a shrill guffaw,
or stoop his head till his eyeballs were almost
hidden beneath their thick lashes, so regard-
ing me for minutes together with a delight-
ful simulation of intelligence, yet with that
peculiar wistful affection his master had him-
self exhibited at first sight of me.

But when our meal was done, Mr. Gulliver
ordered him about his business. Without a
murmur, with one last, long, brotherly glance
at me, he withdrew. And presently after I
heard from afar his high, melancholy "coo-
ee," and the crack of his thong in the after-
noon air as he hastened out to his charges.

My companion did not stir. Only the
flames waved silently along the logs. The
beam of sunlight drew across the floor. The
crisp air of the pasture flowed through the
window. What wonder, then, that, sitting on
my stool, I fell asleep!

Chapter Eight

If I see all, ye're nine to ane!

OLD BALLAD.

I WAS awoke by a sustained sound as of
an orator speaking in an unknown
tongue, and found myself in a sunny-
shadowy loft, whither I suppose I must have
been carried in my sleep. In a delicious
languor between sleeping and waking I lis-
tened with imperturbable curiosity awhile to
that voice of the unknown. Indeed, I was
dozing again when a different sound, enor-
mous, protracted, abruptly aroused me. I
got up hot and trembling, not yet quite my
own master, to discover its cause.

Through a narrow slit between the timbers
I could view the country beneath me, far and
wide. I saw near at hand the cumbrous gate
of the stockade ajar, and at a little distance
on the farther side Mr. Gulliver and his half-

human servant standing. In front of them was an empty space—a narrow semicircle of which Gulliver was the centre. And beyond —wild-eyed, dishevelled, stretching their necks as if to see, inclining their heads as if to hearken, ranging in multitude almost to the sky's verge—stood assembled, it seemed to me, all the horses of the universe.

Even in my first sensation of fear admiration irresistibly stirred. The superb freedom of their unbridled heads, the sun-nurtured arrogance of their eyes, the tumultuous, sea-like tossing of crest and tail, their keenness and ardour and might, and also in simple truth their numbers—how could one marvel if this solitary fanatic dreamed they heard him and understood?

Unarmed, bareheaded, he faced the brutal discontent of his people. Words I could not distinguish; but there was little chance of misapprehending the haughty anguish with which he threatened, pleaded, cajoled. Clear and unfaltering his voice rose and fell. He dealt out fearlessly, foolishly, to that long-snouted, little-brained, wild-eyed multitude, reason beyond their instinct, persuasion beyond their savagery, love beyond their heed.

But even while I listened, one thing I knew those sleek malcontents heard too—the Spirit of man in that small voice of his—perplexed, perhaps, and perverted, and out of tether; but none the less unconquerable and sublime.

What less, thought I, than power unearthly could long maintain that stern, impassable barrier of green vacancy between their hoofs and him? And I suppose for the very reason that these were beasts of a long-sharpened sagacity, wild-hearted, rebellious, yet not the slaves of impulse, he yet kept himself their king who was, in fact, their captive.

"Houyhnhnms?" I heard him cry; "pah —Yahoos!" His voice fell; he stood confronting in silence that vast circumference of restless beauty. And again broke out inhuman, inarticulate, immeasurable revolt. Far across over the tossing host, rearing, leaping, craning dishevelled heads, went pealing and eddying that hostile, brutal voice.

Henry Brocken

Gulliver lifted his hand, and a tempestuous silence fell once more. "Yahoos! Yahoos!" he bawled again. Then he turned, and passed back into his hideous garden. The gate was barred and bolted behind him.

Thus loosed and unrestrained, surged as if the wind drove them, that concourse upon the stockade. Heavy though its timbers were, they seemed to stoop at the impact. A kind of fury rose in me. I lusted to go down and face the mutiny of the brutes; bit, and saddle, and scourge into obedience man's serfs of the centuries. I watched, on fire, the flame of the declining sun upon those sleek, vehement creatures of the dust. And then, I know not by what subtle irony, my zeal turned back—turned back and faded away into simple longing for my lost friend, my peaceful beast-of-evening, Rosinante. I sat down again in the litter of my bed and earnestly wished myself home; wished, indeed, if I must confess it, for the familiar face of my Aunt Sophia, my books, my bed. If these were this land's horses, I thought, what men

might here be met! The unsavouriness, the
solitude, the neighing and tumult and pranc-
ing induced in me nothing but dullness at last
and disgust.

But at length, dismissing all such folly, at
least from my face, I lifted the trap-door and
descended the steep ladder into the room be-
neath.

Mr. Gulliver sat where I had left him.
Defeat stared from his eyes. Lines of insane
thought disfigured his face. Yet he sat, stub-
born and upright, heedless of the uproar,
heedless even that the late beams of the sun
had found him out in his last desolation. So
I too sat down without speech, and waited till
he should come up out of his gloom, and find
a friend in a stranger.

But day waned; the sunlight went out of
the great wooden room; the tumult dimin-
ished; and finally silence and evening shadow
descended on the beleaguered house. And
I was looking out of the darkened window at
a star that had risen and stood shining in the
sky, when I was startled by a voice so low and

so different from any I had yet heard that I turned to convince myself it was indeed Mr. Gulliver's.

"And the people of the Yahoos, Traveller," he said, "do they still lie, and flatter, and bribe, and spill blood, and lust, and covet? Are there yet in the country whence you come the breadless bellies, the sores and rags and lamentations of the poor? Ay, Yahoo, and do vicious men rule, and attain riches; and impious women pomp and flattery?—hypocrites, pandars, envious, treacherous, proud?" He stared with desolate sorrow and wrath into my eyes.

Words in disorder flocked to my tongue. I grew hot and eager, yet by some instinct held my peace. The fluttering of the dying flames, the starry darkness, silence itself; what were we who sat together? Transient shadows both, phantom, unfathomable, mysterious as these.

I fancied he might speak again. Once he started, raised his arm, and cried out as if acting again in dream some frenzy of the past.

And once he wheeled on me extraordinary eyes, as if he half-recognized some idol of the irrevocable in my face. These were momentary, however. Gloom returned to his forehead, vacancy to his eyes.

I heard the outer gate flung open, and a light, strange footfall. So we seated ourselves, all three, for a while, around the smouldering fire. Mr. Gulliver's servant scarcely took his eyes from my face. A little to my confusion, his first astonishment of me had now passed away, and in its stead had fallen such a gentleness and humour as I should not have supposed possible in his wild countenance. He busied himself over his strips of skin, but if he caught my eye upon his own he would smile out broadly, and nod his great, hairy head at me, till I fancied myself a child again and he some vast sweetheart of my nurse.

When we had supped (sitting together in the great room), I climbed the ladder into the loft and was soon fast asleep. But from dreams distracted with confusion I awoke at the first shafts of dawn. I stood beside the narrow window in the wall of the loft and watched the distant river change to silver, the bright green of the grass appear.

This seemed a place of few and timorous birds, and of fewer trees. But all across the dews of the grasses lay a tinge of powdered gold, as if yellow flowers were blooming in abundance there. I saw no horses, no sign of life; heard no sound but the cadent wail of the ash-grey birds in their flights. And when I turned my eyes nearer home, and compared the distant beauty of the forests and their radiant clouds with the nakedness and desolation here, I gave up looking from the window with a determination to be gone as soon as possible from a country so uncongenial.

Moreover, Mr. Gulliver, it appeared, had returned during the night to his first mistrust of my company. He made no sign he saw me, and left his uncouth servant to attend on me. For him, indeed, I began to feel a kind of affection springing up; he seemed so eager to befriend me. And whose is the heart quite hardened against a simple admiration? I rose very gladly when, after having stuffed a wallet with food, he signed to me to follow him. I turned to Mr. Gulliver and held out my hand.

"I wish, sir, I might induce you to accompany me," I said. "Some day we would win our way back to the country we have abandoned. I have known and loved your name, sir, since first I browsed on pictures—Being measured for your first coat in Lilliput by the little tailors: Straddling the pinnacled city. Ay, sir, and when the farmers picked you up 'twixt finger and thumb from among their cornstalks . . ."

I had talked on in hope to see his face relax; but he made no sign he saw or heard me. I very speedily dropped my hand and went out. But when my guide and I had advanced about thirty yards from the stockade, I cast a glance over my shoulder towards the house that had given me shelter. It rose, sad-coloured and solitary, between the green and blue. But, if it was not fancy, Mr. Gulliver stood looking down on me from the very window whence I had looked down on him. And there I do not doubt he stayed till his fellow-yahoo had passed across his inhospitable lands out of his sight for ever.

I was glad to be gone, and did not, at first, realise that the least danger lay before us. But soon, observing the extraordinary vigilance and caution my companion showed, I began to watch and hearken, too. Evidently our departure had not passed unseen. Far away to left and to right of us I descried at whiles now a few, now many, swift-moving shapes. But whether they were advancing with us, or gathering behind us, in hope to catch their tyrant alone and unaware, I could not properly distinguish.

Once, for a cause not apparent to me, my guide raised himself to his full height, and, thrusting back his head, uttered a most piercing cry. After that, however, we saw no more for a while of the beasts that haunted our journey.

All morning, till the sun was high, and the

air athrob with heat and stretched like a great
fiddlestring to a continuous, shrill vibration,
we went steadily forward.   And when at last
I was faint with heat and thirst, my compan-
ion lifted me up like a child on to his back
and set off again at his great, easy stride.   It
was useless to protest.   I merely buried my
hands in his yellow hair to keep my balance
in such a camel-like motion.

A little after noon we stayed to rest by a
shallow brook, beneath a cluster of trees
scented, though not in blossom, like an Eng-
lish hawthorn.   There we ate our meal, or
rather I ate and my companion watched, run-
ning out ever and again for a wider survey,
and returning to me like a faithful dog, to
shout snatches of his inconceivable language
at me.

Sometimes I seemed to catch his meaning,
bidding me take courage, have no fear, since
he would protect me.   And once he shaded his
eyes and pointed afar with extreme perturba-
tion, whining or murmuring while he stared.

Again we set off from beneath the sweet-scented shade, and now no doubt remained that I was the object of very hostile evolutions. Sometimes these smooth-hooved battalions would advance, cloudlike, to within fifty yards of us, and, snorting, ruffle their manes and wheel swiftly away; only once more in turn to advance, and stand, with heads exalted, gazing wildly on us till we were passed on a little. But my guide gave them very little heed. Did they pause a moment too long in our path, or gallop down on us but a stretch or two beyond the limit his instinct had set for my safety, he whirled his thong above his head, and his yell resounded, and like a shadow upon wheat the furious companies melted away.

Evidently these were not the foes he looked for, but a subtler, a more indomitable. It was at last, I conjectured, at scent, or sight, or rumour of these that he suddenly swept me on to his shoulders again, and with a great sneeze or bellow leapt off at a speed he had, as yet, given me no hint of.

Looking back as best I could, I began to

discern somewhat to the left of us a numerous herd in pursuit, sorrel in colour, and of a more magnificent aspect than those forming the other bands. It was obvious, too, despite their plunging and rearing, that they were gaining on us—drew, indeed, so near at last that I could count the foremost of them, and mark (not quite callously) their power and fleetness and symmetry, even the sun's gold upon their reddish skins.

Then in a flash my captor set me down, toppled me over (in plain words) into the thick herbage, and, turning, rushed bellowing, undeviating towards their leaders, till it seemed he must inevitably be borne down beneath their brute weight, and so—farewell to summer. But almost at the impact, the baffled creatures reared, neighing fearfully in consort, and at the gibberish hurled back on them by their flame-eyed master, broke in rout, and fled.

Whereupon, unpausing, he ran back to me, only just in time to rescue me from the nearer thunder yet of those who had seized the very acme of their opportunity to beat out my brains.

It was a long and arduous and unequal contest. I wished very heartily I could bear a rather less passive part. But this fearless creature scarcely heeded me; used me like a helpless child, half tenderly, half roughly, displaying ever and again over his shoulder only a fleeting glance of the shallow glories of his eyes, as if to reassure me of his power and my safety.

But the latter, those distant savannahs will bear witness, seemed forlorn enough. My eyes swam with weariness of these crested, earth-disdaining battalions. I sickened of the heat of the sun, the incessant sidelong jolting, the amazing green. But on we went, fleet and stubborn, into ever-thickening danger. How feeble a quarry amid so many hunters!

Two things grew clearer to me each instant. First, that every movement and feint of our pursuers was of design. Not a beast that wheeled but wheeled to purpose; while the main body never swerved, thundered superbly on toward the inevitable end. And next, I perceived with even keener assurance that my guide knew his country and his enemy and his own power and aim as perfectly and consummately; knew, too—this was the end.

Far distant in front of us there appeared to be a break in the level green, a fringe of bushes, rougher ground. For this refuge he was making, and from this our mutinous Houyhnhnms meant to keep us.

There was no pausing now, not a glance behind. His every effort was bent on speed. Speed indeed it was. The wind roared in my ears. Yet above its surge I heard the neighing and squealing, the ever-approaching shudder of hoofs. My eyes distorted all they looked on. I seemed now floating twenty feet in air; now skimming within touch of ground. Now that sorrel squadron behind me swelled and nodded; now dwindled to an extreme minuteness of motion.

Then, of a sudden, a last, shrill pæan rose

high; the hosts of our pursuers paused, billow-like, reared, and scattered—my poor Yahoo leapt clear.

For an instant once again in this wild journey I was poised, as it were, in space, then fell with a crash, still clutched, sure and whole, to the broad shoulders of my rescuer.

When my first confusion had passed away, I found that I was lying in a dense green glen at the foot of a cliff. For some moments I could think of nothing but my extraordinary escape from destruction. Within reach of my hand lay the creature who had carried me, huddled and motionless; and to left and to right of me, and one a little nearer the base of the cliff, five of those sorrel horses that had been chief of our pursuers. One only of them was alive, and he, also, broken and unable to rise—unable to do else than watch with fierce, untamed, glazing eyes (a bloody froth at his muzzle) every movement and sign of life I made.

I myself, though bruised and bleeding, had received no serious injury. But my Yahoo would rise no more. His master was left alone amidst his people. I stooped over him and bathed his brow and cheeks with the water that trickled from the cliffs close at hand. I pushed back the thick strands of matted yellow hair from his eyes. He made no sign. Even while I watched him the life of the poor beast near at hand welled away: he whinnied softly, and dropped his head upon the bracken. I was alone in the unbroken silence.

It seemed a graceless thing to leave the carcasses of these brave creatures uncovered there. So I stripped off branches of the trees, and gathered bundles of fern and bracken, with which to conceal awhile their bones from wolf and fowl. And him whom I had begun to love I covered last, desiring he might but return, if only for a moment, to bid me his strange farewell.

This done, I pushed through the undergrowth from the foot of the sunny cliffs, and after wandering in the woods, came late in the afternoon, tired out, to a ruinous hut.

Henry Brocken

Here I rested, refreshing myself with the unripe berries that grew near by.

I remained quite still in this mouldering hut looking out on the glens where fell the sunlight. Some homely bird warbled endlessly on in her retreat, lifted her small voice till every hollow resounded with her content. Silvery butterflies wavered across the sun's pale beams, sipped, and flew in wreaths away. The infinite hordes of the dust raised their universal voice till, listening, it seemed to me their tiny Babel was after all my own old, far-off English, sweet of the husk.

Fate leads a man through danger to his delight. Me she had led among woods. Nameless though many of the cups and stars and odours of the flowers were to me, unfamiliar the little shapes that gambolled in fur and feather before my face, here dwelt, mummy of all earth's summers, some old ghost of me, sipper of sap, coucher in moss, quieter than dust.

So sitting, so rhapsodising, I began to hear presently another sound—the rich, juicy munch-munch of jaws, a little blunted maybe, which yet, it seemed, could never cry Enough! to these sweet, succulent grasses. I made no sign, waited with eyes towards the sound, and pulses beating as if for a sweetheart. And soon, placid, unsurprised, at her extreme ease, loomed into sight who but my ox-headed Rosinante in these dells, cropping her delightful way along in search of her drowned master.

I could but whistle and receive the slow, soft scrutiny of her familiar eyes. I fancied even her bland face smiled, as might elderliness on youth. She climbed near with bridle broken and trailing, thrust out her nose to me, and so was mine again.

Sunlight left the woods. Wind passed through the upper branches. So, with rain in the air, I went forward once more; not quite so headily, perhaps, yet, I hope, with undiminished courage, like all earth's travellers before me, who have deemed truth potent as modesty, and themselves worth scanning print after.

Chapter Nine

A . . . shop of rarities.

GEORGE HERBERT.

A LITTLE before darkness fell we struck into a narrow road traversing the wood. This, though apparently not much frequented, would at least lead me into lands inhabited, so turning my face to the West, that I might have light to survey as long as any gleamed in the sky, I trudged on. But I went slow enough: Rosinante was lame; I like a stranger to my body, it was so bruised and tumbled.

The night was black, and a thin rain falling when at last I emerged from the interminable maze of lanes into which the wood-road had led me. And glad I was to descry what seemed by the many lights shining from its windows to be a populous village. A gay village also, for song came wafted on the night air, rustic and convivial.

Hereabouts I overtook a figure on foot, who, when I addressed him, turned on me as sharply as if he supposed the elms above him were thick with robbers, or that mine was a voice out of the unearthly hailing him.

I asked him the name of the village we were approaching. With small dark eyes searching my face in the black shadow of night, he answered in a voice so strange and guttural that I failed to understand a word. He shook his fingers in the air; pointed with the cudgel he carried under his arm now to the gloom behind us, now to the homely galaxy before us, and gabbled on so fast and so earnestly that I began to suppose he was a little crazed.

One word, however, I caught at last from all this jargon, and that often repeated with a little bow to me, and an uneasy smile on his white face—"Mishrush, Mishrush!" But whether by this he meant to convey to me his habitual mood, or his own name, I did not learn till afterwards. I stopped in the heavy road and raised my hand.

"An inn," I cried in his ear, "I want lodging, supper—a tavern, an inn!" as if addressing a child or a natural.

He began gesticulating, evidently vain of having fully understood me. Indeed, he twisted his little head upon his shoulders to observe Rosinante gauntly labouring on. " 'Ame!—'ame?" he cried with a great effort.

I nodded.

"Ah!" he cried piteously.

He led me, after a few minutes' journey, into the cobbled yard of a bright-painted inn, on whose signboard a rising sun glimmered faintly gold, and these letters standing close above it—"The World's End."

Mr. "Mishrush" seemed not a little relieved at nearing company after his lonely walk; triumphant, too, at having guided me hither so cunningly. He lifted his nimble cudgel in the air and waved it conceitedly to and fro in time to the song that rose beyond the window. "Fau'ow er Wur'!—Fau'ow er

Wur'!" he cried delightedly again and again
in my ear, eager apparently for my approval.
So we stood, then, beneath the starless sky,
listening to the rich *choragium* of the
"World's End." They sang in unison, sang
with a kind of forlorn heat and enthusiasm.
And when the song was ended, and the roar
of applause over, Night, like a darkened
water whelmed silently in, engulfed it to the
echo:—

> Follow the World—
>   She bursts the grape,
> And dandles man
>   In her green lap;
> She moulds her Creature
>   From the clay,
> And crumbles him
>   To dust away:
>   Follow the World!

> One Draught, one Feast,
>   One Wench, one Tomb;
> And thou must straight
>   To ashes come:

Henry Brocken

> Drink, eat, and sleep;
>> Why fret and pine?
> Death can but snatch
>> What ne'er was thine:
> Follow the World!

It died away, I say, and an ostler softly appeared out of the shadow. Into his charge, then, I surrendered Rosinante, and followed my inarticulate acquaintance into the noise and heat and lustre of the Inn.

It was a numerous company there assembled. But their voices fell to a man on the entry of a stranger. They scrutinised me, not uncivilly, but closely, seeking my badge, as it were, by which to recognise and judge me ever after.

Mr. Mistrust, as I presently discovered my guide's name indeed to be, was volubly explaining how I came into his company. They listened intently to what, so far as I could gather, might be Houyhnhnmish or Double-Dutch. And then, as if to show me to my place forthwith, a great fleshy fellow that sat close beside the hearth this summer evening continued in a loud voice the conversation I had interrupted.

Whereupon Mr. Mistrust with no little confidence commended me in dumb show to the landlady of the Inn, a Mrs. Nature, if I understood him aright. This person was still comely, though of uncertain age, wore cherry ribbons, smiled rather vacantly from vague, wonderful, indescribable eyes that seemed to change colour, like the chameleon, according to that they dwelt on.

I am afraid, as much to my amusement as wonder, I discovered that this landlady of so much apparent *bonhomie* was a deaf-mute. If victuals, or drink, or bed were required, one must chalk it down on a little slate she carried at her girdle for the purpose. Indeed, the absence of two of her three chief senses had marvellously sharpened the remaining one. Her eyes were on all, vaguely dwelling, lightly gone, inscrutable, strangely fascinating. She moved easily and soundlessly (as fat women may), and I doubt if ever mug or pot of any of that talkative throng remained long empty, except at the tippler's reiterated request.

She laid before me an excellent supper on a little table somewhat removed beside a curtained window. And while I ate I watched, and listened, not at all displeased with my entertainment.

The room in which we sat was low-ceiled and cheerful, but rather close after the rainy night-air. Gay pictures beautified the walls. Here a bottle, a cheese, grapes, a hare, a goblet—in a clear brown light that made the guest's mouth water to admire. Here a fine gentleman toasting a simpering chambermaid. Above the chimney-piece a bloated old man in vineleaves that might be Silenus. And over against the door of the parlour what I took to be a picture of Potiphar's wife, she looked out of the paint so bold and beauteous and craftily. Birds and fishes in cases stared glassily—owl and kestrel, jack and eel and gudgeon. All was clean and comfortable as a hospitable inn can be.

But they who frequented it interested me much more—as various and animated a gathering as any I have seen. Yet in some peculiar manner they seemed one and all not to the last tittle quite of this world. They were, so to speak, more earthy, too definite, too true to the mould, like figures in a bleak, bright light viewed out of darkness. Certainly not one of them was at first blush prepossessing. Yet who finds much amiss with the fox at last, though all he seems to have be cunning?

Near beside me, however, sat retired a man a little younger and more at his ease than most of the many there, and as busy with his eyes and ears as I. His name, I learned presently, was Reverie; and from him I gathered not a little information regarding the persons who talked and sipped around us.

He told me at whiles that his house was not in the village, but in a valley some few miles distant across the meadows; that he sat out these bouts of argument and slander for the sheer delight he had in gathering the myriad strands of that strange rope Opinion; that he lived (heart, soul, and hope) well-nigh alone; that he deeply mistrusted this place, and the company we were in, yet not for its mistress's sake, who was at least faithful to her instincts, candid to the candid, made no favourites, and, eventually, compelled order. He told me also that if friends he had, he deemed it wiser not to name them, since the least sibilance of the sound of the voice incites to treachery; and in conclusion, that of all men he was ac-quainted with, one at least never failed to right his humour; and that one was yonder flabby, pallid fellow with the velvet collar to his coat, and the rings on his fingers, and the gold hair, named Pliable, who sat beside Mr. Stubborn on the settle by the fire.

When, then, I had finished my supper, I drew in my chair a little closer to Mr. Rev-erie's and, having scribbled my wants on the Landlady's slate, turned my attention to the talk.

At the moment when I first began to listen attentively they seemed to be in heated dis-

pute concerning the personal property of a
certain Mr. Christian, who was either dead
or had inexplicably disappeared. Mr. Ob-
stinate, I gathered, had taken as his right this
Christian's "easy-chair"; a gentleman named
Smoothman most of his other goods for a
debt; while a Parson Decorum had appro-
priated as heretical his books and various
peculiar MSS.

But there now remained in question a tri-
fling sum of money which a Mr. Liar loudly
demanded in payment of an "affair of hon-
our." This, however, he seemed little likely
to obtain, seeing that an elderly uncle by
marriage of Christian's, whose name was
Office, was as eager and affable and frank
about the sum as he was bent on keeping it;
and rattled the contents of his breeches'
pocket in sheer bravado of his means to go
to law for it.

"He left a bare pittance, the merest pit-
tance," he said. "What could there be of
any account? Christian despised money,

professed to despise it. That alone would prove my wretched nephew queer in the head —despised *money!*"

"Tush, friend!" cried Obstinate from his corner. "Whether the money is yours, or neighbour Liar's—and it is as likely as not neither's—that talk about despising money's what but a silly lie? 'Twas all sour grapes —sour grapes. He had cunning enough for envy, and pride enough for shame; and at last there was nought but cunning left wherewith to patch up a clout for him and his shame to be gone in. I watched him set out on his pestilent pilgrimage, crazed and stubborn, and not a groat to call his own."

"Yet I have heard say he came of a moneyed stock," said Pliable. "The Sects of Privy Opinion were rare wealthy people, and they, so 'tis said, were his kinsmen. Truth is, for aught I know, Christian must have been in some degree a very liberal rascal, with all his faults." He tittered.

"Oh! he was liberal enough," said Mr. Malice suavely: "why, even on setting out, he emptied his wife's purse into a blind beggar's hat!—his that used to bleat, 'Cast thy bread—cast thy bread upon the waters!' whensoever he spied Christian stepping along the street. They say," he added, burying his clever face in his mug, "the Heavenly Jerusalem lieth down by the weir."

"But we must not contemn a man for his poverty, neighbours," said Liar, gravely composing his hairless face. "Christian's was a character of beautiful simplicity—beautiful! *How* many rickety children did he leave behind him?"

A shrill voice called somewhat I could not quite distinguish, for at that moment a youth rose abruptly near by, and went hastily out.

Obstinate stared roundly. "Thou hast a piercing voice, friend Liar!"

"I did but seek the truth," said Liar.

"But whether or no, Christian believed in it—verily he seemed to believe in it. Was it not so, neighbour Obstinate?" inquired Pliable, stroking his leg.

129

"Believed in what, my friend?" said Obstinate, in a dull voice.

"About Mount Zion, and the Crowns of Glory, and the Harps of Gold, and such like," said Pliable uneasily—"at least, it is said so; so 'tis said."

"Believed!" retorted a smooth young man who seemed to feel the heat, and sat by the staircase door. "That's an easy task—to believe, sir. Ask any pretty minikin!"

"And I'd make bold to inquire of yonder Liveloose," said a thick, monotonous voice (a Mr. Dull's, so Reverie informed me), "if mebbe he be referring to one of his own, or that fellow Sloth's devilish fairy tales? I know one yet he'll eat again some day."

At which remark all laughed consumedly, save Dull.

"Well, one thing Christian had, and none can deny it," said Pliable, a little hotly, "and that was Imagination. *I* shan't forget the tales he was wont to tell: what say you, Superstition?"

Mr. Superstition lifted dark, rather vacant

eyes on Pliable. "Yes, yes," he said: "Flame, and sigh, and lamentation. My God, my God, gentlemen!"

"Oo-ay, Oo-ay," yelped the voice of Mistrust, startled out of silence.

"Oo-ay," whistled Malice, under his breath.

"Tush, tush!" broke in Obstinate again, and snapped his fingers in the air. "And what is this precious Imagination? Whither doth it conduct a man, but to beggary, infamy, and the mad-house? Look ye to it, friend Pliable! 'Tis a devouring flame; give it but wind and leisure, the fairest house is ashes."

"Ashes; ashes!" mocked one called Cruelty, who had more than once taken my attention with his peculiar contortions—"talking of ashes, what of Love-the-log Faithful, Master Tongue-stump? What of Love-the-log Faithful?"

At which Liveloose was so extremely amused, the tears stood in his eyes for laughing.

I looked round for Mistrust, and easily rec-

131

ognised my friend by his hare-like face, and
the rage in his little active eyes. But unfor-
tunately, as I turned to inquire somewhat of
Reverie, Liveloose suddenly paused in his
merriment with open mouth; and the whole
company heard my question, "But who was
Love-the-log Faithful?"

I was at once again the centre of attention,
and Mr. Obstinate rose very laboriously from
his settle and held out a great hand to me.

"I'm pleased to meet thee," he said, with
a heavy bow. "There's a dear heart with
my good neighbour Superstition yonder who
will present a very fair account of that mis-
guided young man. Madam Wanton, here's
a young gentleman that never heard tell of
our old friend Love-the-log."

A shrill peal of laughter greeted this sally.

"Why, Faithful was a young gentleman,
sir," explained the woman, civilly enough,
"who preferred his supper hot."

"Oh, Madam Wanton, my dear, my dear!"
cried a long-nosed woman nearly helpless
with amusement.

I saw Superstition gazing darkly at me. He shook his head as I was about to reply, so I changed my retort. "Who, then, was Mr. Christian?" I inquired simply.

At that the house shook with the roar of laughter that went up.

Chapter Ten

. . . Large draughts of intellectual day.
RICHARD CRASHAW.

"BELIEVE me, neighbours," said Malice softly, when this uproar was a little abated, "there is nought so strange in the question. It meaneth only that this young gentleman hath not enjoyed the pleasure of your company before. Will it amaze you to learn, my friends, that Christian is like to be immortal only because you *talk* him out of the grave? One brief epitaph, gentlemen, would let him rot."

"Nay, but I'll tell the gentleman who Christian was, and with pleasure," cried a lucid, rather sallow little man that had sat quietly smiling and listening. "My name, let me tell you, is Atheist, sir; and Christian was formerly a very near neighbour of an old friend of my family's—Mr. Sceptic.

They lived, sir—at least in those days—opposite to one another."

"He is a great talker," whispered Reverie in my ear. But the company evidently found his talk to their taste. They sat as still and attentive around him as though before an extemporary preacher.

"Well, sir," continued Atheist, "being, in a sense, neighbours, Christian in his youth would often confide in my friend; though, assuredly, Sceptic never sought his confidences. And it seemeth he began to be perturbed and troubled over the discovery that it is impossible—at least in this plain world—to eat your cake, yet have it. And by some ill chance he happened at this time on a mouldy old folio in my friend's house that had been the property of his maternal grandmother—the subtlest old tome you ever set eyes on, though somewhat too dark and extravagant and heady for a sober man of the world like me. 'Twas called the Bible, sir—a collection of legends and fables of all times, tongues, and countries threaded together, mighty ingeniously I grant, and in as plausible a style as any I know, if a little lax and flowery in parts.

"Well, Christian borroweth the book of my friend—never to return it. And being feeble and credulous, partly by reason of his simple wits, and partly by reason of the sad condition a froward youth had reduced him to, he accepts the whole book—from Apple to Vials —for truth. In fact, 'he ate the little book,' as one of the legendary kings it celebrates had done before him."

"Ay," broke in Cruelty wildly, "and has ever since gotten the gripes."

Atheist inclined his head. "Putting it coarsely, gentlemen, such was the case," he said. "And away at his wit's end he hasteneth, wailing and shivering, to a great bog or quagmire—that my friend Pliable will answer to—and plungeth in. 'Tis the same story repeated. He could be temperate in nought. *I* knew the bog well; but I knew the stepping-stones better. Believe me, I have traversed the narrow way this same

Christian took, seeking the harps and pearls and the *elixir vitæ,* these many years past. The book inciteth ye to it. It sets a man's heart on fire—that's weak enough to read it —with its pomp, and rhetoric, and far-away promises, and lofty counsels. Oh, fine words, who is not their puppet! I climbed 'Difficulty.' I snapped my fingers at the grinning Lions. I passed cautiously through the 'Valley of the Shadow'—wild scenery, sir! I visited that prince of bubbles also, Giant Despair, in his draughty castle. And— though boasting be far from me!—fetched Liveloose's half-brother out of a certain charnel-house near by.

"Thus far, sir, I went. But I have not yet found the world so barren of literature as to write a book about it. I have not yet found the world so barren of ingratitude as to seek happiness by stabbing in the back every friend I ever had. I have not yet forsaken wife and children; neighbours and kinsmen; home, ease, and tenderness, for a whim, a dream, a passing qualm. No, sir;

'tis this Christian's ignorant hardness-of-heart
that is his bane. Knowing little, he prateth
much. He would pinch and contract the
Universe to his own fantastical pattern. He
is tedious, he is pragmatical, and—I affirm
it in all sympathy and sorrow—he is crazed.
Malice, haply, is a little sharp at times. And
neighbour Obstinate dealeth full weight with
his opinions. But this Christian Flown-to-
Glory, as the urchins say, pinks with a blud-
geon. He cannot endure an honest doubt.
He distorteth a mere difference of opinion
into a roaring Tophet. And because he is
helpless, solitary, despised in the world; be-
cause he is impotent to refute, and too stub-
born to hear and suffer people a little higher
and weightier, a leetle wiser than he—why,
beyond the grave he must set his hope in
vengeance. Beyond the grave—bliss for his
own shade; fire and brimstone, eternal woe
for theirs. Ay, and 'tis not but for a season
will he vex us, but for ever, and for ever, and
for ever—if he knoweth in the least what he

meaneth by the phrase. And this he calls 'Charity.'

"Yes, sirs, beyond the grave he would condemn us, beyond the grave—a place of peace whereto I deem there are not many here but will be content at length to come; and I not least content, when my duty is done, my children provided for, and my last suspicion of fear and folly suppressed.

"To conclude, sir—and beshrew me, gentlemen, how time doth fly in talk!—this Christian goeth his way. We, each in accord with his caprice and conscience, go ours. We envy him not his vapours, his terrors, or his shameless greed of reward. Why, then, doth he envy us our wealth, our success, our gaiety, our content? He raves. He is haunted. What is man but as grass, and the flower of grass? Come the sickle he is clean gone. I can but repeat it, sir, our poor neighbour was crazed: 'tis Christian in a word."

A sigh, a murmur of satisfaction and relief, rose from the company, as if one and all had escaped by Mr. Atheist's lucidity out of a very real peril.

I thanked him for his courtesy, and in some confusion turned to Reverie with the remark that I thought I now recollected to have heard Christian's name, but understood he had indeed arrived, at last, at the Celestial City for which he had set out.

"Celestial twaddle, sir!" cried Mr. Obstinate hoarsely. "He went stark, staring mad, and now is dust, as we shall soon all be, that's certain."

Then Cruelty rose out of his chair and elbowed his way to the door. He opened it and looked out.

"I would," he said, "I had known of this Christian before he started. Step you down to Vanity Fair, Sir Stranger, if the mood take you; and we'll show you as pretty a persuasion against pilgrimage as ever you saw." He opened his mouth where he stood between me and the stars. ". . . There's many more!" he added with difficulty, as if his rage was too much for him. He spat into the air and went out.

Presently after Liveloose rose up, smiling softly, and groped after him.

A little silence followed their departure.

"You must tell your friend, Mr. Reverie," said Atheist good-humouredly, "that Mr. Cruelty says more than he means. To my mind he is mistaken—too energetic; but his intentions are good."

"He's a staunch, dependable fellow," said Obstinate, patting down the wide cuffs he wore.

But even at that moment a stranger softly entered the inn out of the night. His face was of the grey of ashes, and he looked once round on us all with a still, appalling glance that silenced the words on my lips.

We sat without speech—Obstinate yawning, Atheist smiling lightly, Superstition nibbling his nails, Reverie with chin drawn a little back, Pliable bolt upright, like a green and white wand, Mistrust blinking his little thin lids; but all with eyes fixed on this

141

stranger, who deemed himself, it seemed, among friends.

He turned his back on us and sipped his drink under the heedless, deep, untroubled gaze of Mrs. Nature, and passed out softly and harmlessly as he had come in.

Reverie stood up like a man surprised and ill at ease. He turned to me. "I know him only by repute, by hearsay," he said with an effort. "He is a stranger to us all, indeed, sir—to all."

Obstinate, with a very flushed face, thrust his hand into his breeches' pocket. "Nay, sir," he said, "my purse is yet here. What more would you have?"

At which Pliable laughed, turning to the women.

I put on my hat and followed Reverie to the door.

"Excuse me, sir," I said, "but I have no desire to stay in this house over-night. And if you would kindly direct me to the nearest way out of the village, I will have my horse saddled now and be off."

And then I noticed that Superstition stood in the light of the doorway looking down on us.

"There's Christian's way," he said, as if involuntarily. . . .

"Lodge with me to-night," Reverie answered, "and in the morning you shall choose which way to go you will."

I thanked him heartily and turned in to find Rosinante.

The night was now fine, but moist and sultry, and misty in the distance. It was late, too, for few candles gleamed beneath the moonlight from the windows round about the smooth village-green. Even as we set out, I leading Rosinante by her bridle, and Superstition on my left hand, out of heavenly Leo a bright star wheeled, fading as it fell. And soon high hedges hid utterly the "World's End" behind us, out of sight and sound.

I observed when the trees had laid their burdened branches overhead, and the thick-flowered bushes begun to straiten our way, that this Mr. Superstition, who had desired to accompany us, was of a very different courage from that his manner at the inn seemed to profess.

He walked with almost as much caution and ungainliness as Mistrust, his deep and shining eyes busily searching the gloom to left and right of him. Indeed, those same dark eyes of his reminded me not a little of Mrs. Nature's, they were so full of what they could not tell.

He was on foot; my new friend Reverie, like myself, led his horse, a pale, lovely creature with delicate nostrils and deep-smouldering eyes.

"You must think me very bold to force my company on you," said Superstition awkwardly, turning to Reverie, "but my house is never so mute with horror as in these moody summer nights when thunder is in the air. See there!" he cried.

As if the distant sky had opened, the large, bright, harmless lightning quivered and was gone, revealing on the opposing hills forest above forest unutterably dark and still.

"Surely," I said, "that is not the way Christian took?"

"They say," Reverie answered, "the Valley of the Shadow of Death lies between those hills."

"But Atheist," I said, *"that* acid little man, did he indeed walk there alone?"

"I have heard," muttered Superstition, putting out his hand, " 'tis fear only that maketh afraid. Atheist has no fear."

"But what of Cruelty," I said, "and Live-loose?"

"Why," answered Superstition, "Cruelty works cunningest when he is afraid; and Live-loose never talks about himself. None the less there's not a tree but casts a shadow. I met once an earnest yet very popular young gentleman of the name of Science, who explained almost everything on earth to me so clearly, and patiently, and fatherly, I thought I should evermore sleep in peace. But we met at noon. Believe me, sir, I would have followed Christian and his friend Hopeful

very willingly long since; for as for Cruelty
and Obstinate, and all that clumsy rabble, I
heed them not. Indeed my cousin Mistrust
did go, and as you see returned with a cau-
tion; and a poor young school-fellow of mine,
Jack Ignorance, came to an awful end. But
it is because I owe partly to Christian and not
all to myself this horrible solitude in which I
walk that I dare not risk a deeper. It would
be, I feel sure. And so I very willingly be-
held Faithful burned; it restored my confi-
dence. And here, sir," he added, almost with
gaiety, "lives my friend Mrs. Simple, a
widow. She enjoys my company and my old
fables, and we keep the blinds down against
these mountains, and candles burning against
the brighter lightnings."

So saying, Superstition bade us good-night
and passed down a little by-lane on our left
towards a country cottage, like a dreaming
bower of roses beneath the moon.

But Reverie and I continued on as if the
moon herself as patiently pursued us. And
by-and-by we came to a house called Gloom,

Henry Brocken

whose gardens slope down with plashing
fountains and glimmering banks of flowers
into the shadow and stillness of a broad valley,
named beneath the hills of Silence, Peace.

Chapter Eleven

His soul shall taste the sadness of her might,
And be among the cloudy trophies hung.
JOHN KEATS.

EVEN as we entered the gates of Mr. Reverie's house beneath embowering chestnuts, there advanced across the moonlit spaces to meet us a figure on foot like ourselves, leading his horse. He was in armour, yet unarmed. His steel glittered cold and blue; his fingers hung ungauntleted; and on his pale face dwelt a look never happy warrior wore yet. He seemed a man Mars lends to Venus out of war to unhappy idleness. The disillusionment of age was in his face: yet he was youthful, I suppose; scarce older than Mercutio, and once, perhaps, as light of wit.

He took my hand in a grasp cold and listless, and smiled from mirthless eyes.

148

Yet there was something strangely taking n this solitary knight-at-arms. She for vhom he does not fight, I thought, must have omewhat of the immortals to grace her war- ior with. And if it were only shadows that)eset him and obscured his finer heart, shad-)ws they were of myrtle and rhododen- lron with voices shrill and small as the parrows', and eyes of the next-to-morning tars.

Indeed, these gardens whispered, and the vind at play in the air seemed to bear far- .way music, dying and falling.

We entered the house and sat down to sup-)er in a low room open to the night. Rev- :rie recounted our evening's talk. "I wish," le said, turning to his friend, "you would ac- :ompany Mr. Brocken and me one night to he 'World's End' to hear these fellows talk. 5uch arrogance, such assurance, such bigotry nd blindness and foxiness!—yet, on my word,

kind of gravity with it all, as if the scare- :rows had some real interest in the devil's ares they guard. Come now, let it be a bargain between us, and leave this endless search awhile."

But the solitary knight shook his head. "They would jeer me out of knowledge," he said. "Why, Reverie, the children cease their play when I pass, and draw their tops and marbles out of the dust, and gaze till I am hid from sight."

"It is fancy, only fancy," replied Reverie; "children stare at all things new to them in the world. How else could they recognise and learn again—how else forget? But as for this rabble's mockery, there is a she-bear left called Oblivion which is their mistress, and will some day silence every jeer."

The solitary knight shook his head again, eyeing me solemnly as if in hope to discern in my face the sorcery that held himself in thrall.

The few wax tapers gave but light enough to find the way from goblet to mouth. As for Reverie's wine, I ask no other, for it had the poppy's scarlet, and overcame weariness so subtly I almost forgot these were the hours

of sleep we spent in waking; forgot, too, as if
of the lotus, all thought of effort and hope.

After all, thought I as I sipped, effort is
the flaw that proves men mortal; while as for
hope, who would seek a seed that floats on
every wind and smothers the world with
weeds that bear no fruit? It was, in fact,
fare very different from the ale and cheese of
the "World's End."

"But you yourself," I said to Mr. Reverie
presently; "in all the talk at the inn you kept
a very scrupulous silence—discreet enough,
I own. But now, what truly *was* this Chris-
tian of whom we heard so much? and why,
may I ask, do his neighbours slander the
dead? You yourselves, did you ever meet
with him?" I turned from one to the other
of my companions as they glanced uneasily
each at each.

"Well, sir," said Reverie rather deliber-
ately, "I have met him and talked with him.
I often think of him, in spite of myself. Yet
he was a man of little charm. He certainly
had a remarkable gift for estranging his

friends. He was a foe to the most innocent compromise. For myself, I found not much humour in him, no eye for grace or art, and a limited imagination that was yet his absolute master. Nevertheless, as you hint, these fellows, no more than I, can forget him. Nor you?" He turned to the other.

"Christian," he replied, "I remember him. We were friends a little while. Faithful I knew also. Faithful was to the last my friend. Ah! Reverie, then—how many years ago!— there was a child we loved, all three: do you remember? I see the low, green wall, cool from how many a summer's shadows, the clusters of green apples on the bough. And in the early morning we would go, carrying torn-off branches, and shouting our songs through the fields, till we came to the shadow and the hush of the woods. Ay, Reverie, and we would burst in on silence, each his heart beating, and play there. And perhaps it was Hopeful who would steal away from us, and the others play on; or perhaps you—into the sunlight that maddened the sheltered bird to

flit and sing in the orchard where the little
child we loved played—not yet sad, but how
much beloved; not yet weary of passing shad-
ows, and simple creatures, and boy's rough
gifts and cold hands. But I—with me it was
ever evening, when the blackbird bursts
harshly away. Then it was so still in the
orchard, and in the curved bough so solitary,
that the nightingale, cowering, would almost
for fear begin to sing, and stoop to the bend-
ing of the bough, her sidelong eyes in shade;
while the stars began to stand in the stations
above us, ever bright, and all the night was
peace. Then would I dream on, dream of
the face I loved; Innocence, O Innocence!"

It was a strange outburst. His voice rose
almost to a chant, full of a forlorn music.
But even as he ceased, we heard in the fol-
lowing silence, above the plashing of the
restless fountains, beyond, far and faint, a
wild and stranger music welling. And I saw
from the porch that looks out from the house
called Gloom, "La belle Dame sans Merci"
pass riding with her train, who rides in beauty

Henry Brocken

beneath the huntress, heedless of disguise. Across from far away, like leaves of autumn, skirred the dappled deer. The music grew, timbrel and pipe and tabor, as beneath the glances of the moon the little company sped, transient as a rainbow, elusive as a dream. I saw her maidens bound and sandalled, with all their everlasting flowers; and advancing soundless, unreal, the silver wheels of that unearthly chariot amid the Fauns. On, on they gambolled, hoof in yielding turf, blowing reed melodies, mocking water, their lips laid sidelong, their eyes aleer along the smoothness of their flutes.

And when I turned again to my companions, with I know not what old folly in my eyes, I know not what unanswerable cry in my heart, Reverie alone was at my side. I seemed to see the long fringes of the lake, the sedge withered, the grey waters restless in the bonds of the wind, tuneless and chill; all these happy gardens swept bare and flowerless; and the far hills silent in the unattainable dawn.

"She pipes, he follows," said Reverie;
"she sets the tune, he dances. Yet, sir, on my
soul, I believe it is the childish face of that
same Innocence we kept tryst with long ago
he pursues on and on, through what sad laby-
rinths we, who dream not so wildly, cannot
by taking thought come to guess."

. . . . . .

The next two days passed serenely and
quietly at Reverie's. We read together, rode,
walked, and talked together, and listened in
the evening to music. For a sister of Rev-
erie's lived not far distant, who visited him
while I was there, and took supper with us,
delighting us with her wit and spirit and her
youthful voice.

But though Reverie more than once sug-
gested it, I could not bring myself to return
to the "World's End" and its garrulous com-
pany. Whether it was the moist, grey face
of Mr. Cruelty I most abhorred, or Stub-
born's slug-like eye, or the tongue-stump of
my afflicted guide, I cannot say.

Moreover, I had begun to feel a very keen

curiosity to see the way that had lured Christian on with such graceless obstinacy. They had spoken of remorse, poverty, pride, world-failure, even insanity, even vice: but these appeared to me only such things as might fret a man to set violently out on, not to persist in such a course; or likelier yet, to abandon hope, to turn back from heights that trouble or confusion set so far, and make seem dreams.

How could I help, too, being amused to think how vastly strange these fellows considered a man's venturing whither his star beckoned; though that star were only power, only fame, only beauty, only peace? What wonder they were many?

Not far from this place, Reverie informed me, were pitched the booths of Vanity Fair. This, by his account, was a place one ought to visit, if only for the satisfaction of leaving it behind. But I have heard more animated accounts of it elsewhere.

As for Reverie himself, he seemed only desirous to contemplate; never to taste, to win, or to handle. He needed but refuse reality to what shocked or teased him, to find it harmless and entertaining. He was a dreamer whom the heat and shout of battle could not offend.

Perhaps he perceived my restlessness to be gone, for he himself suggested that I should stay till the next morning, and then, if I so pleased, he would see me a mile or two on my way.

"For the Pitiless Lady," he said, smiling, "takes many disguises, sometimes of the sun, sometimes of evening, sometimes of night; and I would at least save you from the fate that has made my poor friend a phantom before he is a shade."

Chapter Twelve

The many men, so beautiful!
And they all dead did lie.

S. T. COLERIDGE.

SO Reverie, as he had promised, rode out
with me a few miles to see me on my
way. Above the gloom and stillness of
the valley the scene began to change again.
I was glad as I could be to view once more
the tossing cornfields and the wind at play
with shadow. Near and far, woods and pas-
tures smoked beneath the sun. I know not
through how many arches of the elms and
green folds of the meadows I kept watch on
the chimneys of a farmhouse above its trees.

But Reverie, the further we journeyed, the
less he said. I almost chafed to see his heed-
less eyes turned upon some inward dream,
while here, like life itself, stood cloud and
oak, warbled bird and brook beneath the

158

burning sun. I saw again in memory the silver twilight of the moon, and the crazy face of Love's Warrior, haunter of shade. Let him but venture into the open, I thought, hear again the distant lowing of the oxen, the rooks cawing in the elms, see again the flocks upon the hillside!

I suppose this was her home my heart had turned to. This was my dust; night's was his. For me the wild rose and the fields of harvest; for him closed petals, the chantry of the night wind, phantom lutes and voices. And, as if he had overheard my thoughts, Reverie turned at the crossways.

"You will come back again," he said. "They tell me in distant lands men worship Time, set up a shrine to him in every street, and treasure his emblem next their hearts. There, they say, even the lover babbles of hours, and the dreamer measures sleep with a pendulum. Well, my house is secluded, and the world is far; and to me Time is nought. Return, sir, then, when it pleases you. Besides," he added, smiling faintly, "there is always company at the World's End."

The crisp sunbeams rained upon his pale and delicate horse, its equal-plaited mane, on the darkness of his cloak, that dream-delighted face. Here smouldered gold, here flushed crimson, and here the curved damask-ening of his bridle glistened and gleamed. He was a strange visitant to the open day, be-tween the green hedges, beneath the enor-mous branching of the elms. And there I bade him farewell.

Some day, perhaps, I shall return as he has foretold, for it is ever easy to find again the house of Reverie—to them who have learned the way.

On I journeyed, then, following as I had been directed the main road to Vanity Fair. But whether it is that the Fair is more diffi-cult to arrive at than to depart from, or is really a hard day's journey even from the gay parlour of the World's End, it already began to be evening, and yet no sign of bunt-ing or booth or clamour or smoke.

And it was at length to a noiseless Fair, far from all vanity, that I came at sunset—the cypresses of a solitary graveyard. I was tired out and desired only rest; so dismounting and leading Rosinante, I turned aside willingly into its peace.

It seemed I had entered a new earth. The lane above had wandered on in the gloaming of its hedges and over-arching trees. Here, all the clouds of sunset stood, caught up in burning gold. Even as I paused, dazzled a moment by the sudden radiance, from height to height the wild bright rose of evening ran. Not a tottering stone, black, well-nigh shapeless with age, not a green bush, but seemed to dwell unconsumed in its own fire above this desolate ground. The trees that grew around me—willow and yew, thorn and poplar—were but flaming cages for the wild birds that perched in their branches.

Above these sound-dulled mansions trod lightly, as if of thought, Rosinante's gilded shoes. I wandered on in a strange elation of mind, filled with a desperate desire ever to remember how flamed this rose between earth and sky, how throbbed this jargon of delight. And turning as if in hope to share my enthusiasm, a childish peal of laughter showed me I was not alone.

Beneath a canopy of holly branches and yew two children sat playing. The nearer child's hair was golden, glistening round his face of roses, and he it was who had laughed, tumbling on the sward. But the face of the further child was white almost as crystal, and the dark hair that encircled his head with its curved lines seemed as it were the shadow of the gold it showed beside. These children, it was plain, had been running and playing across the tombs; but now they were stooping together at some earnest sport. To me, even if they had seen me, they as yet paid no heed.

I passed slowly towards them, deeming them at first of solitude's creation, my eyes dazzled so with the sun. But as I approached, so the branches beneath which they played gradually disparted, and I saw not far distant from them one sitting who evidently had these jocund boys in charge.

I could not but hesitate awhile as I surveyed them. These were no mortal children playing naked amid the rose of evening: nor she who sat veiled and beautiful beneath the ruinous tombs. I turned with sudden dismay to depart from their presence unobserved as I had entered; but the children had now espied me, and came running, filled with wonder of Rosinante and the stranger beside her.

They stayed at a little distance from us with dwelling eyes and parted lips. Then the fairer and, as it seemed to me, elder of the brothers stooped and plucked a few blades of grass and proffered them, half fearfully, to the beast that amazed him. But the other gave less heed to Rosinante, fixed the filmy lustre of his eyes on me, his wonderful young face veiled with that wisdom which is in all children, and of an immutable gravity.

But by this time, she who it seemed had the charge of these children had followed them with her eyes. To her then, leaving

Rosinante in an ecstasy of timidity before such god-like boys, I addressed myself.

So might a traveller lost beneath strange stars address unanswering Night. She, however, raised a compassionate face to me and listened with happy seriousness as to a child returned in safety at evening from some foolhardy venture. Yet there seemed only a deeper youthfulness in her face for all its eternity of brooding on her beauteous children. Narrow leaves of olive formed her chaplet. The darker wine-colours of the sea changed in her eyes. There was no sense of gloom or sorrowfulness in her company. I began to see how the same still breast might bear celestial children so diverse as these, whose names, she told me presently, were Sleep and Death.

I looked at the two children at play. "Ah! now," I said, almost involuntarily, "the golden boy who has caught my horse's bridle in his hand, is not he Sleep? and he who considers his brother's boldness—that one is Death?"

She smiled with lovely vanity, and told me
how strange of heart young children are.
How they will alter and vary, never the same
for long together, but led by indiscoverable
caprices and obedient to some further will.
She smiled and said how that sometimes,
when the birds hush suddenly from song,
Sleep would creep tenderly and sadly to her
knees, and Death clasp her roguishly, as if in
some secret with the beams of morning. So
would they change, one to the likeness of the
other. But Sleep was, perhaps, of the gen-
tler disposition; a little obstinate and head-
strong; at times, indeed, beyond all cajolery;
yet very sweet of impulse and ardent to make
amends. But Death's caprices baffled even
her. He seemed now so pitiless and unlovely
of heart; and now, as if possessed, passionate
and swift; and now would break away burn-
ing from her arms in an infinite tenderness.

But best she loved them when there came
a transient peace to both; and looking upon
them laid embraced in the shadow-casting
moonbeam, not even she could undoubtingly

165

touch the brow of each beneath their likened hair, and say this is the elder, and this the dreamless younger of the boys.

Seeing, too, my eyes cast upon the undecipherable letters of the tomb by which we sat, she told me how that once, near before dawn, she had awoke in the twilight to find their places empty where the children had lain at her side, and had sought on, at last to find them even here, weeping and quarrelling, and red with anger. Little by little, and with many tears, she had gleaned the cause of their quarrel—how that, like very children, they had run a race at cock-crow, and all these stones and the slender bones and ashes beneath to be the prize; and how that, running, both had come together to the goal set, and both had claimed the victory.

"Yet both seem happy now to share it," I said, "or how else were they comforted?" Nor did I consider before she told me that they will run again when they be grown men, Sleep and Death, in just such a thick darkness before dawn; and one called Love will

then run with them, who is very vehement
and fleet of foot, and never turns aside, nor
falters. He who then shall win may ask a
different prize. For truth to tell, she said,
only children can find delight for long in dust
and ruin.

At that moment Death himself came
hastening to his mother, and, taking her hand,
turned to the enormous picture of the skies as
if in some faint apprehension. But Sleep
saw nothing amiss, lay at full length among
the "cool-rooted flowers," while Rosinante
grazed beside him.

I told her also, in turn, of my journey; and
that although transient, or everlasting, solace
of all restlessness and sorrow and too-wild
happiness may be found in them, yet men
think not often on these divine children.

"As for this one," I said, looking down
into the pathless beauty of Death's grey eyes,
"some fear, some mock, some despise him;
some violently, some without complaint pur-
sue; most men would altogether dismiss, and
forget him. He is but a child, no older than

the sea, no stranger than the mountains, pure and cold as the water-springs. Yet to the bolster of fever his vision flits; and pain drags a heavy net to snare him; and silence is his echoing gallery; and the gold of Sleep his final veil. They shall play on; and see, lady, flame has left the clouds; the birds are at rest. The earth breathes in, and it is day; and exhales her breath, and it is night. Let them then play secret and innocent between her breasts, comfort her with silence above the tempest of her heart. . . . But I!—what am I?—a traveller, footsore and far."

And then it was that I became conscious of a warm, sly, youthful hand in mine, and turned, half in dread, to see only happy Sleep laughing under his glistening hair into my eyes. I strove in vain against his sorcery; rolled foolish orbs on that pure, starry face; and then I smelled as it were rain, and heard as it were tempestuous forest-trees—fell asleep among the tombs.

Chapter Thirteen

I warmed both hands before the fire of life.
WALTER SAVAGE LANDOR.

SURELY some hueless poppy blossomed in the darkness of those ruins, or the soulless ashes of the dead breathe out a drowsy influence. Never have I slept so heavily, yet never perhaps beneath so cold a tester. Sunbeams streaming between the crests of the cypresses awoke me. I leapt up as if a hundred sentinels had shouted—where none kept visible watch.

An odour of a languid sweetness pervaded the air. There was no wind to stir the dew-besprinkled trees. The old, scarred grave-stones stood in a thick sunshine, afloat with bees. But Rosinante had preferred to survey sunshine out of shade. In lush grass I found her, the picture of age, foot crook'd, and head dejected.

169

Henry Brocken

Yet she followed me uncomplaining along these narrow avenues of silence, and without more ado turned her trivial tail on Death and his dim flocks, and well-nigh scampered me off into the vivid morning. Soon afterwards, with Hunger in the saddle, we began to climb a road almost precipitous, and stony in the extreme. Often enough we breathed ourselves as best we could in the still, sultry air, and rested on the sun-dappled slopes. But at length we came out upon the crest, and surveyed in the first splendour of day a region of extraordinary grandeur.

Beneath a clear sky to the east stood a range of mountains, cold and changeless beneath their snows. At my feet a great river flowed, broken here and there with isles in the bright flood. The dark champaign that flanked its shores was of an unusual verdure. Mystery and peril brooded on those distant ravines, the vapours of their far-descending cataracts. In such abysmal fastnesses as these the Hyrcan tiger might hide his surly generations. This was an air for the sun-disdaining eagle, a country of transcendent brightness, its flowers strangely pure and perfect, its waters more limpid, its grazing herds, its birds, its cedar trees, the masters of their kind.

Yet not on these nearer glories my eyes found rest. But, with a kind of heartache, I gazed—as it were towards home—upon the distant waters of the sea. Here, on the crest of this green hill, was silence. There, too, was profounder silence on the sea's untrampled floor. Whence comes that angel out of nought whispering into the ear strange syllables? I know not; but so seemed I to be—a shattered instrument in the 'world, past all true music, o'er which none the less the invisible lute-master stooped. Could I but catch, could I but in words express the music his bent fingers intended, the mystery, the peace—well; then I should indeed journey solitary on the face of the earth, a changeling in its cities.

I half feared to descend into a country so diverse from any I had yet seen. Hitherto at least I had encountered little else than friendliness. But here—doves in eyries! I stood, twisting my fingers in Rosinante's mane, debating and debating. And she turned her face to me, and looked with age into my eyes: and—I know not how—woke courage in me again.

"On then?" I said, on the height. And the gentle beast leaned forward and coughed into the valley what might indeed be "Yea!"

So we began to descend. Down we went, alone, yet not unhappy, until in a while I discovered, about a hundred yards in advance of me, another traveller on the road, ambling easily along at an equal pace with mine. I know not how far I followed in his track debating whether to overtake and to accost him, or to follow on till a more favourable chance offered.

But Chance—avenger of all shilly-shally —settled the matter offhand. For my traveller, after casting one comprehensive glance towards the skies, suddenly whisked off at a canter that quickly carried him out of sight.

A chill wind had begun to blow, lifting in

gusts dust into the air and whitening the tree-
tops. As suddenly, calm succeeded. A
cloud of flies droned fretfully about my ears.
And I watched advancing, league-high, trans-
figured with sunbeams, the enormous gloom
of storm. The sun smote from a silvery haze
upon its peaks and gorges. Wind, far above
the earth, moaned, and fell; only to sound
once more in the distance in a mournful
trumpeting. Lightnings played along the
desolate hills. The sun was darkened. A
vast flight of snowy, arrow-winged birds
streamed voiceless beneath his place. And
day withdrew its boundaries, spread to the
nearer forests a bright amphitheatre, fitful
with light, whereof it seemed to me Rosinante
with her poor burden was the centre and the
butt. I confess I began to dread lest even
my mere surmise of danger should engage
the piercing lightnings; as if in the mystery
of life storm and a timorous thought might
yet be of a kin.

We hastened on at the most pathetic of gal-
lops. Nor seemed indeed the beauteous

lightning to regard at all that restless mote upon the cirque of its entranced fairness. In an instantaneous silence I heard a tiny beat of hoofs; in instantaneous gloom recognised almost with astonishment my own shape bowed upon the saddle. It was a majestic entry into a kingdom so far-famed.

The storm showed no abatement when at last I found shelter. From far away I had espied in the immeasurable glare a country barn beneath trees. Arrived there, I almost fell off my horse into as incongruous and light-hearted a company as ever was seen.

In the midst of the floor of the barn, upon a heap of hay, sat a fool in motley blowing with all his wind into a pipe. It was a cunning tune he played too, rich and heady. And so seemed the company to find it, dancers—some thirty or more—capering round him with all the abandon heart can feel and heel can answer to. As for pose, he whose horse now stood smoking beside my own first drew my attention—a smooth, small-bearded, solemn man, a little beyond his prime. He lifted his toes with such inimitable agility, postured his fingers so daintily, conducted his melon-belly with so much elegance, and exhaled such a warm joy in the sport that I could look at nothing else at first for delight in him.

But there were slim maids too among the plumper and ruddier, like crocuses, like lilac, like whey, with all their fragrance and freshness and lightness. Such eyes adazzle dancing with mine, such nimble and discreet ankles, such gimp English middles, and such a gay delight in the mere grace of the lilting and tripping beneath rafters ringing loud with thunder, that Pan himself might skip across a hundred furrows for sheer envy to witness.

As for the jolly rustics that were jogging their wits away with such delightful gravity, but little time was given me to admire them ere I also was snatched into the ring, and found brown eyes dwelling on mine, and a hand like lettuces in the dog-days. Round and about we skipped in the golden straw, amidst treasuries of hay, puffing and spinning. And the quiet lightnings quivered between the beams, and the monstrous "Ah!" of the thunder submerged the pipe's sweetness. Till at last all began to gasp and blow indeed, and the nodding Fool to sip, and sip, as if *in extremis* over his mouthpiece. Then we rested awhile, with a medley of shrill laughter and guffaws, while the rain streamed lightning-lit upon the trees and tore the clouds to tatters.

With some little circumstance my traveller picked his way to me, and with a grave civility bowed me a sort of general welcome. Whereupon ensued such wit and banter as made me thankful when the opening impudence of a kind of jig set the heels and the petticoats of the company tossing once more. We danced the lightning out, and piped the thunder from the skies. And by then I was so faint with fasting, and so deep in love with at least five young country faces, that I scarcely knew head from heels; still less, when a long draught of a kind of thin, sweet ale had mounted to its sphere.

Away we all trooped over the flashing fields, noisy as jays in the fresh, sweet air, some to their mowing, some to their milking, but more, indeed, I truly suspect, to that exquisite *Nirvana* from which the tempest's travail had aroused them. I waved my hand, striving in vain to keep my eyes on one blest, beguiling face of all that glanced behind them. But, she gone, I turned into the rainy lane once more with my new acquaintance, discreeter, but not less giddy, it seemed, than I.

We had not far to go—past a meadow or two, a low green wall, a black fish-pool— and soon the tumbledown gables of a house came into view. My companion waved his open fingers at the crooked casements and peered into my face.

"Ah!" he said, "we will talk, we will talk, you and I: I view it in your eye, sir—clear and full and profound—such ever goes with eloquence. 'Tis my delight. What are we

177

else than beasts?—beasts that perish? I
never tire; I never weary;—give me to dance
and to sing, but ever to talk: then am I at
ease. Heaven is just. Enter, sir—enter!"

He led me by a shady alley into his or-
chard, and thence to a stable, where we left
Rosinante at hob-nob with his mare over a
friendly bottle of hay. And we ourselves
passed into the house, and ascended a stair-
case into an upper chamber. This chamber
was raftered, its walls hung with an obscure
tapestry, its floor strewn with sand, and its
lozenged casement partly shuttered against
the blaze of sunshine that flowed across the
forests far away to the west.

My friend eyed me brightly and busily as
a starling. "You danced fine, sir," he said
"Oh! it is a *pleasure* to me. Ay, and now
I come to consider it, methought I did hear
hoofs behind me that might yet be echo. No,
but I did *not* think: 'twas but my ear cried to
his dreaming master. Ever dreaming; God
help at last the awakening! But well met,
well met, I say again. I am cheered. And

you but just in time! Nay, I would not have missed him for a ransom. So: so: this leg, that leg; up now—hands over—down we go! Lackaday, I am old bones for such freaks. Once! . . . *Memento mori!* say I, and smell the shower the sweeter for it. Be seated, sir, bench or stool, wheresoever you'd be. You're looking peaked. That burden rings in my skull like a bagpipe. Toot-a-tootie, toot-a-toot! Och, sad days!"

We devoured our meal of cold meats and pickled fish, fruit and junket and a kind of harsh cheese, as if in contest for a wager. And copious was the thin spicy wine with which we swam it home. Ever and again my host would desist to whistle, or croon (with a packed mouth) in the dismallest of tenors, a stave or two of the tune we had danced to, bobbing head and foot in sternest time. Then a great vacancy would overspread his face turned to the window, as suddenly to gather to a cheerful smile, and light, irradiated, once more on me. Then down would drop his chin over his plate, and away go finger and

179

spoon among his victuals in a dance as brisk and whole-hearted as the other.

He took me out again into his garden after supper, and we walked beneath the trees.

" 'Tis bliss to be a bachelor, sir," he said, gazing on the resinous trunk of an old damson tree. "I gorge, I guzzle; I am merry, am melancholy; studious, harmonical, drowsy —and none to scold or deny me. For the rest, why, youth is vain: yet youth had pleasure—innocence and delight. I chew the cud of many a peaceful acre. Ay, I have nibbled roses in my time. But now, what now? I have lived so long far from courts and courtesy, grace and fashion, and am so much my own close and indifferent friend—Why! he is happy who has solitude for housemate, company for guest. I say it, I say it; I marry daily wives of memory's fashioning, and dream at peace."

It seemed to be an old bone he picked with Destiny.

"There's much to be said," I replied as profoundly as I could.

The air he now lulled youth asleep with was a very cheerless threnody, but he brightened once more at praise of his delightful orchard.

"You like it, sir? You speak kindly, sir. It is my all; root and branch: how many a summer's moons have I seen shine hereon! I know it—there is bliss to come;—miraculous Paradise for men even dull as I. Yet 'twill be strange to me—without my house and orchard. Age tends to earth, sir, till even an odour may awake the dead—a branch in the air call with its fluttering a face beyond Time to vanquish dear. 'Soul, soul,' I cry, 'forget thy dust, forget thy vaunting ashes!'—and speak in vain. So's life!"

And when we had gone in again, and candles had been lit in his fresh and narrow chamber, seeing a viol upon a chest, I begged a little music.

He quite eagerly, with a boyish peal of laughter, complied; and sat down with a very solemn face, his brows uplifted, and sang be-

181

tween the candles to a pathetic air this dog-
gerel :—

> There's a dark tree and a sad tree,
> Where sweet Alice waits, unheeded,
> For her lover long-time absent,
> Plucking rushes by the river.

> Let the bird sing, let the buck sport,
> Let the sun sink to his setting;
> Not one star that stands in darkness
> Shines upon her absent lover.

> But his stone lies 'neath the dark tree,
> Cold to bosom, deaf to weeping;
> And 'tis gathering moss she touches,
> Where the locks lay of her lover.

"A dolesome thing," he said; "but my
mother was wont to sing it to the virginals.
'Cold to bosom,'" he reiterated with a plan-
gent cadence; "I remember them all, sir;
from the cradle I had a gift for music." And
then, with an ample flirt of his bow, he broke,
all beams and smiles, into this ingenuous
ditty:—

Henry Brocken

The goodman said,
" 'Tis time for bed,
Come, mistress, get us quick to pray;
    Call in the maids
    From out the glades
  Where they with lovers stray,
  With love, and love do stray."

  "Nay, master mine,
  The night is fine,
And time's enough all dark to pray;
    'Tis April buds
    Bedeck the woods
Where simple maids away
With love, and love do stray.

  "Now we are old,
  And nigh the mould,
'Tis meet on feeble knees to pray;
    When once we'd roam,
    'Twas else cried, 'Come,
And sigh the dusk away,
With love, and love to stray.' "

  So they gat in
  To pray till nine;

Then called, "Come maids, true maids, away!
   Kiss and begone,
   Ha' done, ha' done,
  Until another day
  With love, and love to stray!"

   Oh, it were best
   If so to rest
Went man and maid in peace away!
   The throes a heart
   May make to smart
  Unless love have his way,
  In April woods to stray!—
  In April woods to stray!

And that finished with another burst of laughter, he set very adroitly to the mimicry of beasts and birds upon his frets. Never have I seen a face so consummately the action's. His every fibre answered to the call; his eyebrows twitched like an orator's; his very nose was plastic.

"Hst!" he cried softly; "hither struts chanticleer!" "Cock-a-diddle-doo!" crowed the wire. "Now, prithee, Dame Partlett!" and

184

down bustled a hen from an egg like cinnamon. A cat with kittens mewed along the string, anxious and tender.

"A woodpecker," he cried, directing momentarily a sedulous, clear eye on me. And lo, "inviolable quietness" and the smooth beech-boughs! "And thus," he said, sitting closer, "the martlets were wont to whimper about the walls of the castle of Inverness, the castle of Macbeth."

"Macbeth!" I repeated—"Macbeth!"

"Ay," he said, "it was his seat while yet a simple soldier—flocks and flocks of them, wheeling hither, thither, in the evening air, crying and calling."

I listened in a kind of confusion. ". . . And Duncan," I said. . . .

He eyed me with immense pleasure, and nodded with brilliant eyes on mine.

"What looking man was he?" I said at last as carelessly as I dared. ". . . The King, you mean—of Scotland."

He magnanimously ignored my confusion, and paused to build his sentence.

" 'Duncan'?" he said. "The question calls him straight to mind. A lean-locked, womanish countenance; sickly, yet never sick; timid, yet most obdurate; more sly than politic. An *ignis fatuus,* sir, in a world of soldiers." His eye wandered. . . . " 'Twas a marvellous sanative air, crisp and pure; but for him, one draught and outer darkness! I myself viewed his royal entry from the gallery—pacing urbane to slaughter; and I uttered a sigh to see him. 'Why, sir, do you sigh to see the king?' cried one softly that stood by. 'I sigh, my lord,' I answered to the instant, 'at sight of a monarch even Duncan's match!' "

He looked his wildest astonishment at me.

"Not, I'd have you remember—not that 'twas blood I did foresee. . . . To kill in blood a man, and he a king, so near to natural death . . . foul, foul!"

"And Macbeth?" I said presently—"Macbeth . . . ?"

He laid down his viol with prolonged care. "His was a soul, sir, nobler than his fate.

I followed him not without love from boyhood—a youth almost too fine of spirit; shrinking from all violence, over-nicely; eloquent, yet chary of speech, and of a dark profundity of thought. The questions he would patter!—unanswerable, searching earth and heaven through. . . . And who now was it told me the traitor Judas's hair was red?—yet not red his, but of a reddish chestnut, fine and bushy. Children have played with harmless hands at hide-and-seek therein. O sea of many winds!

"For come gloom on the hills, floods, discolouring mist; breathe but some grandam's tale of darkness and blood and doubleness in his hearing: all changed. Flame kindled; a fevered unrest drove him out; and Ambition, that spotted hound of hell, strained at the leash towards the Pit.

"So runs the world—the ardent and the lofty. We are beyond earth's story as 'tis told, sir. All's shallower than the heart of man. . . . Indeed, 'twas one more shattered altar to Hymen."

187

" 'Hymen'!" I said.

He brooded long and silently, clipping his small beard. And while he was so brooding, a mouse, a moth, dust—I know not what, stirred the listening strings of his viol to sound, and woke him with a start.

"I vowed, sir, then, to dismiss all memory of such unhappy deeds from mind—never to speak again that broken lady's name. Oh! I have seen sad ends—pride abased, splendour dismantled, courage to terror come guilt to a crying guilelessness."

" 'Guilelessness'?" I said. "Lady Macbeth at least was past all changing."

The doctor stood up and cast a deep scrutiny on me, which yet, perhaps, was partly on himself.

"Perceive, sir," he said, "this table—broader, longer, splendidly burdened; and all adown both sides the board, thanes and their ladies, lords, and gentlemen, guests bidden to a royal banquet. 'Twas then in that bleak and dismal country—the Palace of Forres. Torches flared in the hall; to every man a servant or two: we sat in pomp."

He paused again, and gravely withdrew behind the tapestry.

"And presently," he cried therefrom, suiting his action to the word, "to the blast of hautboys enters the king in state thus, with his attendant lords. And with all that rich and familiar courtesy of which he was master in his easier moods he passed from one to another, greeting with supple dignity on his way, till he came at last softly to the place prepared for him at table. And suddenly— shall I ever forget it, sir?—it seemed silence ran like a flame from mouth to mouth as there he stood, thus, marble-still, his eyes fixed in a leaden glare. And he raised his face and looked once round on us all with a forlorn astonishment and wrath, like one with a death-wound—I never saw the like of such a face.

"Whereat, beseeching us to be calm, and pay no heed, the queen laid her hand on his and called him. And his orbs rolled down once more upon the empty place, and stuck as if at grapple with some horror seen within. He muttered aloud in peevish altercation— once more to heave up his frame, to sigh and shake himself, and lo!——"

The viol-strings rang to his "lo!"

"Lo, sir, the Unseen had conquered. His lip sagged into his beard, he babbled with open mouth, and leaned on his lady with such an impotent and slavish regard as I hope never to see again man pay to woman. . . . We thought no more of supper after that. . . .

"But what do I——?" The doctor laid a cautioning finger on his mouth.

"The company was dispersed, the palace gloomy with night (and they were black nights at Forres!), and on the walls I heard the sentinel's replying. . . . In the wood's last glow I entered and stood in his self-same station before the empty stool. And even as I stood thus, my hair creeping, my will con- centred, gazing with every cord at stretch, fell a light, light footfall behind me." He glanced whitely over his shoulder.

"Sir, it was the queen come softly out of slumber on my own unquiet errand."

The doctor strode to the door, and peered out like a man suspicious or guilty of treachery. It was indeed a house of broken silences. And there, in the doorway, he seemed to be addressing his own saddened conscience.

"With all my skill, and all a leal man's gentleness, I solaced and persuaded, and made an oath, and conducted her back to her own chamber unperceived. How weak is sleep! . . . It was a habit, sir, contracted in childhood, long dormant, that Evil had woke again. The Past awaits us all. So run Time's sands, till mercy's globe is empty and . . ."

He stooped and whispered it across to me: ". . . A child, a comparative child, shrunk to an anatomy, her beauty changed, ghostly of youth and all its sadness, baffled by a word, slave to a doctor's nod! None knew but I, and, at the last, one of her ladies—a gentle, faithful, and fearful creature. Nor she till far beyond all mischief. . . .

"Wild deeds are done. But to have blood on the hands, a cry in the ears, and one same glassy face eye to eye, that nothing can dim, nor even slumber pacify—dreams, dreams, intangible, enorm! Forefend them, God, from me!"

He stood a moment as if he were listening; then turned, smiling irresolutely, and eyed me aimlessly. He seemed afraid of his own house, askance at his own furniture. Yet, though I scarce know why, I felt he had not told me the whole truth. Something fidelity had yet withheld from vanity. I longed to inquire further. I put aside how many burning questions awhile!

Chapter Fourteen

And if we gang to sea, master,
I fear we'll come to harm.

OLD BALLAD.

B Y-AND-BY less anxious talk soothed him. Indeed it was he who suggested one last bright draught of air beneath his trees before retiring. Down we went again with some unnecessary clatter. And here were stars between the fruited boughs, silvery Capella and the Twins, and low on the sky's moonlit border Venus excellently bright.

He asked me whither I proposed going, if I needs must go; besought there and then in the ambrosial night-air the history of my wanderings—a mere nine days' wonder and told me how he himself much feared and hated the sea.

He questioned me also with not a little

subtilty (and double-dealing too, I fancied) regarding my own country, and of things present, and things "real." In fact nothing, I think, so much flattered his vanity—unless it was my wonder at Dame Partlett's clucking on his viol-strings—as to learn himself was famous even so far as to ages yet unborn. He gazed on the simple moon with limpid, amiable eyes, and caught my fingers in his.

How, then, could I even so much as hint to inquire which century indeed was his, who had no need of any? How could I abash that kindly vanity of his by adding also that, however famous, he must needs be to all eternity —nameless?

We conversed long and earnestly in the coolness. He very frankly counselled me not to venture unconducted further into this country. The land of Tragedy was broad. And though on this side it lay adjacent to the naïve and civil people of Comedy, on the further, in the shadow of those bleak, unfooted mountains, lurked unnatural horror and desolation, and cruelty beyond all telling.

He very kindly offered me too, if I was indeed bent on seeking the sea, an old boat, still seaworthy, that lay in a creek in the river near by, from which he was wont to fish. As for Rosinante, he supposed a rest would be by no means unwelcome to so faithful a friend. He himself rode little, being indolent, and a happier host than guest; and when I returned here, she should be stuffed with dainties awaiting me.

To this I cordially and gratefully agreed; and also even more cordially to remain with him the next day; and the next night after that to take my watery departure.

So it was. And a courteous, versatile, and vivacious companion I found him. Rarer tales he told me, too, of better days than these, and rarest of his own nevermore-returning youth. He loved his childhood, talked on of it with an artless zeal, his eyes a nest of singing birds. How contrite he was for spirit lost, and daring withheld, and hope discomfited! How simple and urbane concerning his present lowly demands on life, on love, and on futurity! All this, too, with such packed winks and mirth and mourning, that I truly said good-night for the second time to him with a rather melancholy warmth, since to-morrow . . . who can face unmoved that viewless sphinx? Moreover, the sea is wide, has fishes in plenty, but never too many coraled grottoes once poor mariners.

Chapter Fifteen

'Tis now full tide 'tween night and day.
                                JOHN WEBSTER.

ON the stroke of two next morning the doctor conducted me down to the creek in the river-bank where he kept his boat. There was little light but of the stars in the sky; nothing stirring. She floated dim and monstrous on the softly-running water, a navy in germ, and could have sat without danger thirty men like me. We stood on the bank, side by side, eyeing her vacancy. And (I can answer for myself) night-thoughts rose up in us at sight of her. Was it indeed only wind in the reeds that sighed around us? only the restless water insistently whispering and calling? only of darkness were these forbidding shadows?

I looked up sharply at the doctor from such pensive embroidery, and found him as far away as I. He nodded and smiled, and we shook hands on the bank in the thick mist.

"There's biscuits and a little meat, wine, and fruit," he said in an undertone. "God be with you, sir! I sadly mistrust the future. . . . 'Tis ever my way, at parting."

We said good-bye again, to the dream-cry of some little fluttering creature of the rushes. And well before dawn I was floating midstream, my friend a memory, Rosinante in clover, and my travels, so far as this brief narrative will tell, nearly ended.

I saw nothing but a few long-haired, grazing cattle on my voyage, that eyed me but cursorily. I passed unmolested among the waterfowl, between the never-silent rushes, beneath a sky refreshed and sweetened with storm. The boat was enormously heavy and made slow progress. When too the tide began to flow I must needs push close in to the bank and await the ebb. But towards evening of the third day I began to approach the sea.

I listened to the wailing of its long-winged gulls; snuffed with how broad-nostrilled a gusto that savour not even pinewoods can match, nor any wild flower disguise; and heard at last the sound that stirs beneath all music—the deep's loud-falling billow.

I pushed ashore, climbed the sandy bank, and moored my boat to an ash tree at the waterside. And after scrambling some little distance over the dunes yet warm with the sun, I came out at length, and stood like a Greek before the sea.

Here my bright river disembogued in noise and foam. Far to either side of me stretched the faint gold horns of a bay; and beyond me, almost violet in the shadow of its waves, the shipless sea.

I looked on the breaking water with a divided heart. Its light, salt airs, its solitary beauty, its illimitable reaches seemed tidings of a region I could remember only as one who, remembering that he has dreamed, remembers nothing more. Larks rose, singing, behind me. In a calm, golden light my eager river quarrelled with its peace. Here indeed was solitude.

It was in searching sea and cliff for the least sign of life that I thought I descried on the furthest extremity of the nearer of the horns of the bay the spires and smouldering domes of a little city. If I gazed intently, they seemed to vanish away, yet still to shine above the azure if, raising my eyes, I looked again.

So, caring not how far I must go so long as my path lay beside these breaking waters, I set out on the firm, white sands to prove this city the mirage I deemed it.

What wonder, then, my senses fell asleep in that vast lullaby! And out of a day-dream almost as deep as that in which I first set out, I was suddenly aroused by a light tapping sound, distinct and regular between the roaring breakers.

I lifted my eyes to find the city I was seeking evanished away indeed. But nearer at hand a child was playing upon the beach, whose spade among the pebbles had caused the birdlike noise I had heard.

So engrossed was she with her building in the sand that she had not heard me approaching. She laboured on at the margin of the cliff's shadow where the sea-birds cried, answering Echo in the rocks. So solitary and yet so intent, so sedate and yet so eager a little figure she seemed in the long motionlessness of the shore, by the dark heedlessness of the sea, I hesitated to disturb her.

Who of all Time's children could this be playing uncompanioned by the sea? And at a little distance betwixt me and her in the softly-mounded sand her spade had already scrawled in large, ungainly capitals, the answer—"Annabel Lee." The little flounced black frock, the tresses of black hair, the small, beautiful dark face—this then was Annabel Lee; and that bright, phantom city I had seen—that was the vanishing mockery of her kingdom.

I called her from where I stood—"Annabel Lee!" She lifted her head and shook back her hair, and gazed at me startled and intent.   I went nearer.

"You are a very lonely little girl," I said.

"I am building in the sand," she answered.

"A castle?"

She shook her head.

"It was in dreams," she said, flushing darkly.

"What kind of dream was it in then?"

"Oh!   I often dream it; and I build it in the sand.   But there's never time: the sea comes back."

"Was the tide quite high when you began?" I asked; for now it was low.

"Just that much from the stones," she said; "I waited for it ever so long."

"It has a long way to come yet," I said; "you will finish it *this* time, I dare say."

She shook her head and lifted her spade.

"Oh no; it is much bigger, more than twice. And I haven't the seaweed, or the shells, and it comes back very, very quickly."

"But where is the little boy you play with down here by the sea?"

She glanced at me swiftly and surely; and shook her head again.

"He would help you."

"He didn't in my dream," she said doubtfully. She raised long, stealthy eyes to mine, and spoke softly and deliberately. "Besides, there isn't any little boy."

"None, Annabel Lee?" I said.

"Why," she answered, "I have played here years and years and years, and there are only the gulls and terns and cormorants, and that!" She pointed with her spade towards the broken water.

"You know all their names then?" I said.

"Some I know," she answered with a little frown, and looked far out to sea. Then, turning her eyes, she gazed long at me, searchingly, forlornly on a stranger. "I am going home now," she said.

I looked at the house of sand and smiled. But she shook her head once more.

"It never *could* be finished," she said firmly, "though I tried and tried, unless the sea would keep quite still just once all day,

without going to and fro. And then," she
added with a flash of anger—"then I would
not build."

"Well," said I, "when it is nearly finished,
and the water washes up, and up, and washes
it away, here is a flower that came from
Fairyland. And that, dear heart, is none so
far away."

She took the purple flower I had plucked
in Ennui's garden in her slim, cold hand.

"It's amaranth," she said; and I have never
seen so old a little look in a child's eyes.

"And all the flowers' names too?" I said.

She frowned again. "It's amaranth," she
said, and ran off lightly and so deftly among
the rocks and in the shadow that was advanc-
ing now even upon the foam of the sea, that
she had vanished before I had time to deter,
or to pursue her. I sought her awhile, until
the dark rack of sunset obscured the light, and
the sea's voice changed; then I desisted.

It was useless to remain longer beneath the
looming caves, among the stones of so in-
hospitable a shore. I was a stranger to the

tides. And it was clear high-water would submerge the narrow sands whereon I stood.

Yet I cannot describe how loth I was to leave to-night's desolation the shapeless house of a child. What fate was this that had set her to such profitless labour on the uttermost shores of "Tragedy"? What history lay behind, past, or, as it were, never to come? What gladness too high for earth had nearly once been hers? Her sea-mound took strange shapes in the gloom—light foliage of stone, dark heaviness of granite, wherein rumour played of all that restless rustling; small cries, vast murmurings from those green meadows, old as night.

I turned, even ran away, at last. I found my boat in the gloaming where I had left her, safe and sound, except that all the doctor's good things had been nosed and tumbled by some hungry beast in my absence. I stood and thought vacantly of Crusoe, and pig, and guns. But what use to delay? I got in.

If it were true, as the excellent doctor had informed me, that seamen reported islands not far distant from these shores, chance might bear me blissfully to one of these. And if not true . . . I turned a rather startled face to the water, and made haste not to think. Fortune pierces deep, and baits her hooks with sceptics. Away I went, bobbing mightily over the waves that leapt and wrestled where sea and river met. These safely navigated, I rowed the great creature straight forward across the sea, my face towards dwindling land, my prow to Scorpio.

Chapter Sixteen

Art thou pale for weariness?
PERCY BYSSHE SHELLEY.

THE constellations of summer wheeled above me; and thus between water and starry sky I tossed solitary in my boat. The faint lustre of the sultry night hung like a mist from heaven to earth. Far away above the countries I had left perhaps for ever, the quiet lightnings played innocently in the heights.

I rowed steadily on, guiding myself by some much ruddier star on the horizon. The pale phosphorescence on the wave, the simple sounds as of fish stirring in the water—the beauty and wonder of Night's dwelling-place seemed beyond content of mortality.

I leaned on my oars in the midst of the deep sea, and seemed to hear, as it were, the mighty shout of Space. Faint and enormous beams

of light trembled through the sky. And once
I surprised a shadow as of wings sweeping
darkly across, star on to glittering star, shak-
ing the air, stilling the sea with the cold dews
of night.

So rowing, so resting, I passed the mark
of midnight. Weariness began to steal over
me. Between sleep and wake I heard strange
cries across the deep. The thin silver of the
old moon ebbed into the east. A chill mist
welled out of the water and shrouded me in
faintest gloom. Wherefore, battling no more
against such influences, I shipped my oars,
made my prayer in the midst of this dark
womb of Life, and screening myself as best I
could from the airs that soon would be mov-
ing before dawn, I lay down in the bottom of
the boat and fell asleep.

I slept apparently without dream, and woke
as it seemed to the sound of voices singing
some old music of the sea. A scent of a fra-
grance unknown to me was eddying in the
wind. I raised my head, and saw with eyes
half-dazed with light an island of cypress and

poplar, green and still above the pure glass of its encircling waters. Straight before me, beyond green-bearded rocks dripping with foam, a little stone house, or temple, with columns and balconies of marble, stood hushed upon the cliff by the waterside.

All now was soundless. They that sang, whether Nereids or Sirens, had descended to dimmer courts. The seamews floated on the water; the white dove strutted on the ledge; only the nightingales sang on in the thick arbours.

I pushed my boat between the rocks towards the island. Bright and burning though the beams of the sun were, here seemed ever-lasting shadow. And though at my gradual intrusion, at splash or grating of keel, the startled cormorant cried in the air, and with one cry woke many, yet here too seemed per-petual stillness.

How could I know what eyes might not be regarding me from bowers as thick and se-cluded as these? Yet this seemed an isle in some vague fashion familiar to me. To these same watery steps of stone, to this same mooring-ring surely I had voyaged before in dream or other life? I glanced into the water and saw my own fantastic image beneath the reflected gloom of cypresses, and knew at least, though I a shadow might be, this also was an island in a sea of shadows. Far from all land its marbles might be reared, yet they were warm to my touch, and these were nightingales, and those strutting doves beneath the little arches.

So very gradually, and glancing to and fro into these unstirring groves, I came presently to the entrance court of the solitary villa on the cliff-side. Here a thread-like fountain plashed in its basin, the one thing astir in this cool retreat. Here, too, grew orange trees, with their unripe fruit upon them.

But I continued, and venturing out upon the terrace overlooking the sea, saw again with a kind of astonishment the doctor's green, unwieldy boat beneath me and the emerald of the nearer waters tossing above the yellow sands.

Here I had sat awhile lost in ease when I heard a footstep approaching and the rhythmical rustling of drapery, and knew eyes were now regarding me that I feared, yet much desired to meet.

"Oh me!" said a clear yet almost languid voice. "How comes any man so softly?"

Turning, I looked in the face of one how long a shade!

I strove in vain to hide my confusion. This lady only smiled the deeper out of her baffling eyes.

"If you could guess," she said presently, "how my heart leapt in me, as if, poor creature, any oars of earth could bring it ease, you would think me indeed as desolate as I am. To hear the bird scream, Traveller! I hastened from the gardens as if the black ships of the Greeks were come to take me. But such is long ago. Tell me, now, is the world yet harsh with men and sad with women? Burns yet that madness mirth calls Life? or truly does the puny, busy-tongued race sleep at last, nodding no more at me?"

I told as best I could how chance had fetched me; told, too, that earth was yet pestered with men, and heavenly with women. "And the madness mirth calls Life flickers yet," I said; "and the little race tosses on in nightmare."

"Ah!" she replied, "so ever run travellers' tales. I too once trusted to seem indifferent. But you, if shadow deceives me not, may yet return: I, only to the shades whence earth draws me. Meanwhile," she said, looking softly at the fountain playing in the clear gloom beyond, "rest and grow weary again, for there flock more questions to my tongue than spines on the blackthorn. The gardens are green with flowers, Traveller; let us talk where rosemary blows."

Following her, I thought of the mysterious beauty of her eyes, her pallor, her slimness, and that faint smile which hovered between ecstasy and indifference, and away went my mind to one whom the shrewdest and tenderest of my own countrymen called once Criseyde.

She led me into a garden all of faint-hued flowers. There bloomed no scarlet here, nor blue, nor yellow; but white and lavender and purest purple. Here, also, like torches of the sun, stood poplars each by each in the windless air, and the impenetrable darkness of cypresses beneath them.

Here, too, was a fountain whose waters leapt no more, mossy and time-worn. I could not but think of those other gardens of my journey—Jane's, Ennui's, Dianeme's; and yet none like this for the shingley murmur of the sea, and the calmness of morning.

"But, surely," I said, "this must be very far from Troy."

"Far indeed," she said.

"Far also from the hollow ships."

"Far also from the hollow ships," she replied.

"Yet," said I, "in the country whence I come is a saying: Where the treasure is——"

"Alack! *there* gloats the miser!" said Criseyde. "But I, Traveller, have no treasure,

213

only a patchwork memory, and that's a great grief."

"Well, then, forget! Why try in vain?" I said.

She smiled and seated herself, leaning a little forward, looking upon the ground.

"Soothfastness *must,*" she said very gravely, raising her long black eyebrows; "yet truly it must be a forlorn thing to be remembered by one who so lightly forgets. So then I say, to teach myself to be true—'Look now, Criseyde, yonder fine, many-hearted poplar—that is Paris; and all that bank of marriage-ivy—that is marriageable Helen, green and cold; and the waterless fountain—that truly is Diomed; and the faded flower that nods in shadow, why, that must be me, even me, Criseyde!'"

"And this thick rosemary-bush that smells of exile, who, then, is that?" I said.

She looked deep into the shadow of the cypresses. "That," she said, "I think I have forgot again."

"But," I said, "Diomed, now, was he quite

so silent—not one trickle of persuasion?"

"Why," she said, "I think 'twas the fountain was Diomed: I know not. And as for persuasion, he was a man forked, vain, and absolute as all. Let the waterless stone be sudden Diomed—you will confuse my wits, Mariner; where, then, were I?" She smiled, stooping lower. "You have voyaged far?" she said.

"From childhood to this side regret," I answered rather sadly.

" 'Tis a sad end to a sweet tale," she said, "were it but truly told. But yet, and yet, and yet—you may return, and life heals every, every wound. I must look on the ground and make amends. 'Tis this same making amends men now call 'Purgatory,' they tell me."

" 'Amends,' " I said; "to whom? for what?"

"Welaway," said she, with a narrow fork between her brows; "to most men and to all women, for being that Criseyde." She gazed half solemnly at some picture of reverie.

"But which Criseyde?" I said. "She who

215

was every wind's, or but one perfect summer's?"

She glanced strangely at me. "Ask of the night that burns so many stars," she said. "All's done; all passes. Yet my poor busy Uncle Pandar had no such changes, nor Hector, nor . . . Men change not: they love and love again—one same tune of a myriad verses."

"All?" I said.

She tossed lightly a little dust from her hand.

"Nay—all," she replied. "But what is that to me? Mine only to see Charon on the wave pass light over and return. Man of the green world, prithee die not yet awhile! 'Tis dull being a shade. See these cold palms! Yet my heart beats on."

"For what?" I said.

Criseyde folded her hands and leaned her cheek sidelong upon the stone.

"For what?" I repeated.

"For what but idle questions?" she said; "for a traveller's vanity that deems looking love-boys into a woman's eyes her sweeter entertainment than all the heroes of Troy. Oh, for a house of nought to be at peace in! Oh, goosish swan! Oh, brittle vows! Tell me, Voyager, is it not so?—that men are merely angry boys with beards; and women—repeat not, ye who know! Never yet set I these steadfast eyes on a man that would not steal the moon for taper—would she but come down." She turned an arch face to me: "And what is to be faithful?"

"I?" said I—" 'to be faithful'?"

"It is," she said, "to rise and never set, O sun of utter weariness! It is to kindle and never be quenched, O fretting fire of midsummer! It is to be snared and always sing, O shrilling bird of dullness! It is to come, not go; smile, not sigh; wake, never sleep. Could'st *thou* love so many nots to a silk string?"

"And to be fickle?—what is that?" said I.

"Ah! to be fickle," she said, "is showers after drought, seas after sand; to cry, unechoed; to be thirsty, the pitcher broken. And—ask now this pitiless darkness of the eyes!—to be remembered though Lethe flows between. Nay, you shall watch even hope away ere another comes like me to mope and sigh, and play at swords with Memory."

She rose to her feet and drew her hands across her face, and smiling, sighed deeply. And I saw how inscrutable and lovely she must ever seem to eyes scornful of mean men's idolatries.

"And you will embark again," she said softly; "and in how small a ship on seas so mighty! And whither next will fate entice you, to what new sorrows?"

"Who knows?" I said. "And to what further peace?"

She laughed lightly. "Speak not of mockeries," she said, and fell silent.

She seemed to be thinking quickly and deeply; for even though I did not turn to her, I could see in imagination the restless sparkling of her eyes, the stillness of her ringless hands. Then suddenly she turned.

"Stranger," she said, drawing her finger

softly along the cold stone of the bench, "there yet remain a few bright hours to morning. Who knows, seeing that felicity is with the bold, did I cast off into the sea—who knows whereto I'd come! 'Tis but a little way to being happy—a touch of the hand, a lifting of the brows, a shuddering silence. Had I but man's courage! Yet this is a solitary place, and the gods are revengeful."

I cannot say how artlessly ran that voice in this still garden, by some strange power persuading me on, turning all doubt aside, calming all suspicion.

"There is honeycomb here, and the fruit is plenteous. Yes," she said, "and all travellers are violent men—catch and kill meat: *that* I know, however doleful. 'Tis but a little sigh from day to day in these cool gardens; and rest is welcome when the heart pines not. Listen, now; I will go down and you shall show me—did one have the wit to learn, and courage to remember—you shall show me how sails your wonderful little ship; tell me, too, where on the sea's horizon to one in exile earth lies, with all its pleasant things—yet thinks so bitterly of a woman!"

"Tell me," I said, "tell me but one thing of a thousand. Whom would *you* seek, did a traveller direct you, and a boat were at your need?"

She looked at me, pondering, weaving her webs about me, lulling doubt, and banishing fear.

"One could not miss—a hero!" she said, flaming.

"That, then, shall be our bargain," I replied with wrath at my own folly. "Tell me this precious hero's name, and though all the dogs of the underworld come to course me you shall take my boat and leave me here— only this hero's name, a pedlar's bargain!"

She lowered her lids. "It must be Diomed," she said with the least sigh.

"It must be," I said.

"Nay, then, Antenor, or truly Thersites," she said happily, "the silver-tongued!"

"Good-bye, then," I said.

"Good-bye," she replied very gently. "Why, how could there be a vow between us? I go, and return. You await me—me, Criseyde, Traveller, the lonely-hearted. That is the little all, O much-surrendering Stranger! Would that long-ago were now—before all chaffering!"

Again a thousand questions rose to my tongue. She looked sidelong at the dry fountain, and one and all fell silent.

"It is harsh, endless labour beneath the burning sun; storms and whirlwinds go about the sea, and the deep heaves with monsters."

"Oh, sweet danger!" she said, mocking me.

I turned from her without a word, like an angry child, and made my way to the steps into the sea, pulled round my boat into a little haven beside them, and showed her oars and tackle and tiller; all the toil, and peril, the wild chances.

"Why," she cried, while I was yet full of the theme, "I will go then at once, and to-morrow Troy will come."

I looked long at her in silence; her slim

beauty, the answerless riddle of her eyes, the age-long subtlety of her mouth, and gave no more thought to all life else.

Day was already waning. I filled the water-keg with fresh water, put fruit and honeycomb and a pillow of leaves into the boat, proffered a trembling hand, and led her down.

The sun's beams slanted on the foamless sea, glowed in a flame of crimson on marble and rock and cypress. The birds sang endlessly on of evening, endlessly, too, it seemed to me, of dangers my heart had no surmise of.

Criseyde turned from the dark green waves. "Truly, it is a solitary country; pathless," she said, "to one unpiloted"; and stood listening to the hollow voices of the water. And suddenly, as if at the consummation of her thoughts, she lifted her eyes on me, darkly, with unimaginable entreaty.

"What do you seek else?" I cried in a voice I scarcely recognised. "Oh, you speak in riddles!"

I sprang into the boat and seized the heavy

oars. Something like laughter, or, as it were, the clapper of a scarer of birds, echoed among the rocks at the rattling of the rowlocks. As if invisible hands withdrew it from me, the island floated back.

I turned my prow towards the last splendour of the sun. A chill breeze played over the sea: a shadow crossed my eyes.

Buoyant was my boat; how light her cargo! —an oozing honeycomb, ashy fruits, a few branches of drooping leaves, closing flowers; and solitary on the thwart the wraith of life's unquiet dream.

So fell night once more, and made all dim. And only the cold light of the firmament lit thoughts in me restless as the sea on which I tossed, whose moon was dark, yet walked in heaven beneath the distant stars.

Printed in the United Kingdom
by Lightning Source UK Ltd.
107642UKS00001B/135